"To my mind, the lyrics he wrote...are as blinding a display of raw, universe-gobbling intelligence as have ever been penned...The sources from which Chris drew his inspiration are a classic pop cultural blend – exploitation films of all stripes, pulp fiction, French decadent poets, hot rod gangs, mystical Catholicism, underground biker comix, beatnik booze into the hippie acid continuum, and on and on and on. This is a mix that has gained great subterranean currency over the past few decades, but when Chris was churning through these waters, they were as yet uncharted. His written work (along with that of fellow travelers such as Exene Cervenka, Dave Alvin, John Doe and Claude 'Kickboy' Bessy) created a new, totally crazed hipster aesthetic that rejected punk orthodoxy in favor of something much more magnificent and inclusive."

– Byron Coley, writer for WIRE Magazine,
author of C'EST LA GUERRE:
EARLY WRITINGS 1978-1983
and co-author (with Thurston Moore)
of NO WAVE: POST-PUNK.
UNDERGROUND.NEW YORK. 1976-1980.

MOTHER'S WORRY

Mother's Worry

by

Chris D.

A Poison Fang Book

If you enjoy this book, tell someone about it.

A Poison Fang Book

Front and back cover designs by C. D.

ISBN: 978 0615869346

First Poison Fang Books Edition, August 2013

Previously published by New Texture Books in August 2012

Printed in the United States

10 9 8 7 6 5 4 3 2 1

FOR BYRON COLEY AND TOM GIVAN...

I'D ALREADY PLOWED THROUGH
ALL OF HAMMETT, CHANDLER
AND JAMES M. CAIN
BETWEEN LATE HIGH SCHOOL
AND POST-GRAD COLLEGE
BUT, IN THE EARLY 1980S,
BYRON AND TOM TURNED ME ON
TO THE TORMENTED JOYS OF
HARRY CREWS,
DAVID GOODIS,
RICHARD STARK,
DAN J. MARLOWE
AND, ESPECIALLY,
JIM THOMPSON...

FOR BETTER OR WORSE,
IF NOT FOR THESE TWO GOOD FRIENDS,
THERE IS A CHANCE
I MIGHT NEVER HAVE VENTURED
SO FAR DOWN
THIS TWISTED ROAD

PART ONE
Ray Diamond
April 1987

Chapter 1

All afternoon I'd been thinking it'd sure be nice to be lying in Mama's backyard, smelling bacon from the kitchen. Feeling that god-awful but oh-so-homey sensation of Georgia's own personal, smothering death star of a sun making the morning summer air barely breathable. But my house was in a suitcase and would be until I could hitch a ride to Mama's place in Mystic.

It's a hell of a long way from San Diego to Georgia, especially when you're traveling the way I was. And it's a pretty even bet you're not going to get anybody to stop and pick you up when you look like you've just gotten out of the slammer. Which is how I looked, my thumb stuck out in the sweltering July heat when it might as well have been up my ass.

Where I'd been those last two years, there wasn't much difference. Being in the Navy had been almost as bad as any Federal prison. I'd say it was worse, but I'm not impartial enough to make comparisons.

It'd been hell pretty much from the get-go – from the time I'd
been inducted in New Orleans until my last station there outside of
Coronado. The start of the second year marked the halfway point in
that infernal haul – it was right about then the monotonous routine had
taken a turn for the worse.

I'd begun to rub a certain Ensign J.J. Munson the wrong
way. First off, he hadn't liked my mug – the long deep scar I carry on
my left cheek, or how I'd gotten it. He'd laughed condescendingly
because he'd thought I was joking about crazy Lester, the snake-
handling preacher who passes through Mystic once a year, putting on
puppet vs. snake sideshows for the kids when he was sober enough, and
ranting double-talk sermons outside Mystic's only drive-in movie when
he wasn't.

It was one of those nights, a Friday night coming out of a triple
bill of *Gomar The Human Gorilla, Her Flesh Is Weak* and *Curse of the
Brimstone Bed*. My girlfriend Connie Eustace McQueen and I were on
foot because my '57 Chevy was at Jake Platt's getting the transmission
rebuilt. We'd taken a couple of folding lawn chairs along with a quart
of rye and a six-pack. We'd sat out under the stars way in the back,
getting soused then occasionally watching the lunatic stuff up on the
screen when we weren't making out.

When we'd walked out the exit gate after everyone else had
left, Lester had followed us. We were so drunk ourselves we didn't
even notice him until we came along side the DeRosie brothers' south
pasture. Suddenly, he'd jumped from the inky shadows of a poplar into
the moonlight, running at Connie with an itty-bitty coral snake in one
hand and a rusty straight razor in the other. Connie had had enough
sense to hightail it while I stayed behind to return Lester's friendly
overtures. For some strange reason, I can still see Connie's jet-black
hair streaming around her sensual face as she kind of hopped, skipped
backwards out of harm's way.

Lester had dropped the snake when I tripped him. But before I
could break the empty rye bottle over his head, he came at me swinging
the razor in a wide arc, and it connected. As soon as he'd seen the blood
spurting from my cheek, he'd known he'd gone too far. He'd dropped it
and had started running and, if it wasn't for Connie Eustace catching up
to me, I'd sure as hell have killed the loony son-of-a-bitch.

As I said before, Ensign Munson didn't like the story.
Especially not after he found out from my buddy Jack Bride that it was

true. He called me a liar, trying to bait me into a fight. But I kept my cool.

Relations between us that once could've been termed civil quickly deteriorated. Things came to a head one Saturday night outside a little beer joint in Coronado called Deucey The Swinger. I finally took as much as I could stomach and let him have it. I ended up breaking his jaw while Jack, Earl and Ted cheered me on. Afterwards, while we sat on the curb outside chugging beers, Munson slunk off with his tail between his legs and banged the hell out of his custom Hemi trying to maneuver it out of the parking lot. Unfortunately, none of us realized just how nuts old Munson was. The other guys were able to get out of the way in plenty of time. But he smashed my left leg up bad when he ran over me. He came at me so fast, and we were so goddamn blind with whiskey, I'm surprised he didn't nail us all.

I was in the infirmary for over a month before I could even get around on crutches. And while I was there, a "doctor" named Williams gave Munson a run for his money trying to do me in. Not only did he set my leg wrong the first time, he had to have another doctor come all the way down from San Pedro to re-break it and rectify his mistake.

A patient named Harrison who'd been in there at the same time hadn't been so lucky. Williams had operated, yanking out the poor devil's shinbone and replacing it with an artificial one that didn't take. When Harrison had started having fevers, fevers so bad that he'd be raving half-conscious for hours on end or simply screaming his lungs out, shrieking himself hoarse from the unbearable agony, it had finally dawned on Williams that something was seriously wrong. Only it had been too late. Harrison's leg had gangrened, and "Doctor" Williams had failed to catch it in time. Before he could amputate his botched-up experiment, the infection – the blood poisoning, the gangrenous, maggot-infested, slo-mo manifestation of DEATH – spread over Harrison's body like a blanket of putrid, foul-smelling pox. And helpless Harrison died in unbearable pain.

After that, they'd had a hell of a time getting me to even let Williams in the ward without me throwing my bedpan at him.

When I got out, I went over Munson's head, straight to the Admiral to complain about Williams. But because Munson had it in for me more than ever, I didn't get any farther than the Admiral's outer office. I was stalled in the waiting room filling out forms when Munson burst in with some strong-arm MP goons and had them arrest me.

He wanted to get me for breaking his jaw. The bile must've been welling all the way up out of his stomach into his taste buds. The whole bottom half of his face was still wired – unfortunately not shut. He talked in a teeth-grating whisper that made my hair stand on end.

I spent the last two months of my Coronado stay languishing in the stockade. Luckily, Munson had been unable to make Jack and the boys give evidence, so he had to be satisfied with a lowly charge of insubordination. Even then, he had had to ramrod the case through to keep me locked up.

Finally, I was released. My discharge was honorable, much to Munson's shock. I never could be sure, but I figured that I had Jack, Earl and Ted to thank for that. How they managed it, I'll never know.

The day after I was discharged, Doc Williams was arrested for – among other things – gross negligence. It'd been discovered he wasn't really a doctor after all, just some fast-talking conman who'd had papers forged.

So I was still walking with a limp when I hitchhiked out of the base. I wasn't too sure at first what I was going to do or where I was going. I wanted to get back to Mystic. But how long it was going to take and how I was going to get there was a grey area.

I'd been debating heading into mainland Mexico through Mexicali, picking up a kilo of junk from some connections I knew, then hightailing it to New Orleans to get rid of the stuff. That way I'd get back to Mystic with enough scratch to marry Connie Eustace and not have to work for a while.

It was a crazy thing to do, but I reckoned I could handle myself well enough. And I wasn't worried about the karma of dealing with "hard" drugs.

I still had the .45 I'd been issued – records showed I'd turned it in long ago. I'd walked right out of the front gate with it in my bag, and they'd never missed it. I figured it'd take them at least a month or two to realize it was gone, and they'd be hard-pressed to ever prove it was me.

Chapter 2

I changed my mind about Mexicali, but not about Mexico. I took an air-conditioned Greyhound into Arizona, then New Mexico, staying on it as it zigzagged along the U.S. border, enjoying the thunderstorm that seemed to follow us.

The April weather was cool and breezy in El Paso, the only time I'd ever been there when it had been. But there was still a humid blanket over everything that made the 65 degree temperature seem more like 85. The way the locals were acting, I'm sure it must've been setting some kind of record for pleasantness. El Paso's claim to immortality is its heat, dirt and miserable food. For most of the rest of the time I was there – just a couple of days – it seemed to live up to all three.

I took a small room, close to the Mexican border, and I got rid of the suitcase and everything in it – except the .45. The hotel had a climate unto itself, generating a sticky claustrophobic heat that gave the lie to the bearable weather as soon as you opened a window. I had to go down to the 7-11 to pick up some disinfectant spray – that's how bad it smelled.

But I wasn't there for a pleasant time. I wasn't a tourist, and I didn't give a damn about souvenirs. I was there to case a liquor store, a nice, fat little rabbit to hunt down and pluck from the heather before crossing the border. Something to provide financing for my humble drug-dealing plans. Not just any joint. There were scores of just-making-their-rent-type establishments, owner-operated businesses barely making ends meet. As far as I was concerned, they didn't exist. They were strictly off limits. I wanted to find a syndicate-run place that did a large volume, had a bulging till at least two or three days of the week. Something worth the trouble. I didn't want some honest Joe's bread-and-butter, some pathetic working stiff's last nickel. I wanted to cut a bit of fat off the huge prime rib that got served up nice and rare to the big boys in Vegas, Houston and Phoenix twice a week. I knew they were there. It was just a matter of finding the right one.

I finally found what I was looking for towards the end of the second day – a long, narrow joint that started in San Ignacio Street and went straight through to the next block, spilling out onto Vasquez Avenue. Mr. B's Liquors. Run by a fat, white-haired man with a high-blood pressure complexion and rheumy, blue albino eyes. I knew it was the place the minute I lay eyes on him.

He was sitting in a high chair underneath a blinding neon sign. It threw a pale blueness over him, making him look like a corpse fresh out of the morgue. The rest of the place was a maze of shadows, the stacked-to-ceiling aisles giving it the baroque feel of some marketplace from the Dark Ages.

The guy acted nervous the minute he saw me come into the store. There were a bunch of Mex kids playing Centipede by the San Ignacio entrance, making a lot of noise break-dancing to a ghetto blaster in between turns. But that was routine. He may have been a fat slob, but he was smart enough – or had enough of a sixth sense – to know me for what I was. The second I stepped in out of the sunlight, and he could make out more than a silhouette, he started his worrying. I just stood there staring at him, giving him the evil eye.

After ten or twenty seconds, one of the kids slid over on his skateboard and asked me for a quarter. I handed him a dollar bill. His eyes bugged out, and he acted like he was afraid to touch it.

"Go ahead, it won't bite."

"*Gracias, señor.*" He yanked it out of my hand and rolled back between embankments of stale potato chips to the cluttered counter.

"*Señor* Red, change, *por favor.*"

Red ignored him and continued to return my stare. The kid slapped the counter loudly like he was used to getting what he wanted.

"*Señor* Red!"

Red obviously didn't want to give him the time of day, let alone four quarters.

I lazily sauntered over and stood towering over the kid.

"He needs change. I'll buy something, too, if that's what it takes to get your fat ass down off that high chair."

He didn't bat an eye. He raised his pudgy left hand and, for the first time, I saw that he was smoking a cigar. A massive, soggy butt stuck out from between his greasy thumb and forefinger. He sucked a heavy dose of it into his wheezy lungs, then closed his eyes. Suddenly it struck me what he looked like – some bargain basement Buddha ruminating over material problems, a portly redneck guru lost in reverie, meditating on the mundane – and I burst out laughing.

Not trusting his ears, his eyes sprung open. He coughed, and blue clouds of stogie smoke spluttered over the kid's head. The kid made a face and held his nose. Red slumped off his wobbly perch and punched the ancient brass register with his fist, and the drawer popped open. Without breaking eye contact with me, he pinched out four quarters, then tossed them towards the door. The kid shook his head like it was something not unusual. The coins clattered across the brittle, cracked linoleum, and he rocketed after them before his pals could beat him to the punch.

"You're really in the big time, hunh? Making twelve-year-olds jump for chump change. I bet that ain't all the strings you pull."

"What doya want, asshole? You gotta mighty big mouth for just some thirsty joker off the street."

"That's all I am, friend – a thirsty joker. I'd like a pint of Old Overholt and a sixpack of Tecate."

He frowned as he bent over beneath the counter to where he kept his pints. He lay the rye on its side in front of me with his left hand, then – still clutched in his meaty, sweaty right palm – a .357 Magnum right next to it.

"You're a real hotrodder, boy. I hate to be the one to tell you, but this ain't the time or the place."

I smiled.

He motioned with the gun. "We're outta Tecate. The beer's in the back there near the other door, if you want something else. If not, that'll be $4.25, and you can get the fuck outta here."

I looked at him for a few seconds, then headed for the beer fridge. Just before I opened the sliding glass, I spotted a beefy, mullet-headed kid snoring peacefully in a chair beside the rear entrance. He wore a football jersey several sizes too small and sported a silver safety

pin in his right ear. But he could obviously take care of himself. He had
a stylized inscription of "Semper Fi" tattooed on his inner left forearm,
and a huge baseball bat was propped up against a box of cigarette
cartons a couple of feet away.

I picked out a sixpack of Corona and slammed the glass door as
hard as I could, hoping it'd crack.

"That'll be $9.50."

I threw down a ten. "Keep the change – Red."

"Sure. Sure, I'll keep the change, And don't come back in here
again – unless you want that baseball bat you were staring at wrapped
around your skull."

I smiled at him, then headed out into the blinding sunlight of
San Ignacio. There was a hush from the kids, and they stopped their
game of Centipede to look up at me as I walked out. The kid I'd given
the dollar to ran after me.

I didn't stop right away because I didn't want to chance Red
spotting me talking to him. Once I'd gotten about a block, and he was
still tailing me, making a helluva racket with his skateboard's cheap
metal wheels. I turned the corner. He stuck like flypaper. Suddenly, I
stopped, and he piled right into me.

"What's goin' on, pal?"

"*Señor*, nobody ever done that to Red."

"Yeah?"

"I just wanted to shake your hand."

I smiled and took his tiny, dirty palm in mine.

"No one mess with Red. He is one – what do you call it? No-
good bastard. *Muy malo.* That liquor store is a real gangster hangout."

The kid was hip to what was going down, more so than I would
have guessed. He was gabby, too, so I let him run off at the mouth a bit.

"Red and his son, Eli, run the numbers. Take bets for the dog
races, too. *Mucho caliente.* But the cops, they don't even bother them."

"How's that?"

He rolled his eyes. "C'mon, dude, you don't look stupid."

"Well, chief, since you know so much…tell me, when's all the
really big money there?" Maybe I shouldn't have popped the question
so soon or so obviously, but I was thinking, *what the hell?* I'd already
blown my cover as much as I possibly could, swaggering like a real
cock-of-the-walk. It could mean getting my head blown off, but I was
willing to take the chance. The kid stared at me.

"You *loco*?" He turned away, angling his skateboard around so
it pointed back in Mr. B's direction.

"Hold on. I'm willing to pay for the info."

That nailed him in his tracks. He did a 180, a silly grin nearly splitting his face in two. He shrugged and held out his hand again.

"Five dollar."

When I gave it to him without any hesitation, it threw him. He looked at the bill like he wasn't sure it was real. I hadn't even tried to finagle the price down, and it seemed to bother him.

"I never ever met anyone like you, señor. My name is Javier."

"Ray."

"Raymundo?"

"Sure. Whatever you like, kid."

"Raymundo is my godfather's name."

Luckily his godfather was someone he liked. Still, he was getting sidetracked, and I didn't have time for it. The town wasn't that big. Red would undoubtedly get the word out on me as poison, and I wanted to make myself scarce until I knocked the place over. Besides, I couldn't take it too much longer outside in the suddenly building heat and blinding daylight. I'd left my sunglasses and hat back in my room.

"What's the deal on how much dinero goes through the place and when?"

I guess I'd shut him down some, because he looked hurt.

"Look...Javier." I gave him another dollar. "I'm in a hurry. I'm expecting a phone call back at my hotel," I lied.

He shrugged and nodded. Suddenly, he looked like the sad little boy that he was, someone growing up too fast.

"Hey, I used to have a skateboard like that when I was about your age. It had metal wheels, too. It used to drive my old man crazy."

I knew I'd hit a responsive chord with him because his eyes lit up.

"You, too? Mama hates it. I can't even bring it in the house no more. I have to hide it in the garage."

A garage? That made me feel a better. He couldn't be too bad off if his family had a house with a garage. Especially in El Paso. Suddenly, he got serious again, concerned over my timetable.

"Oh, right. You're in a hurry. Whatever you do is okay with me. Especially if Red don't like it, the son-of-a-bitch. He's got the most money, I think, tomorrow afternoon just before the last race at the dog track. He keeps it overnight. But I think there's a lot right now, too..." He winked like he knew exactly what I was up to. "He keeps it in a floor safe behind the counter, by his chair."

I stuck out my hand, and he pumped it wildly.

"You've been *mucho* help, Javier."

"Good luck, *Señor* Ray. I hope your mission is successful."

Then he was halfway down the street, the crummy metal wheels of his skateboard whining obnoxiously over the rutted concrete walk.

Chapter 3

When I got back to my room, I lay on the double bed and stared at the flies playing tag with the ceiling fan.

I tried to figure exactly how I was going to handle hitting Mister B's: the time of day, whether to wear a mask or not, Red and the mullet-head's defensive capabilities, the odds of both mob and/or law enforcement coming after me, and how much time I'd have to get across the border. I was going into this whole thing like an amateur. It'd been a good couple years since I'd pulled any jobs, and there was no getting around it. I was rusty – rusty as hell. But I had to start again somewhere. I reckoned it might as well be Mister B's. All I needed was seven or eight grand, and with their mob ties, they'd probably have it. That'd get me a second-hand car, a quantity of smack and pay my rent at least through New Orleans, probably to Mystic. I knew how to live on a lean budget. My connection was inexpensive, but good Indian farmers growing, harvesting and refining opium poppies as cash crop in a valley hidden from the Federales, as well as other cartels and the clientele. It had been a while since I'd been in touch, and that kind of business can change, even disappear, overnight, especially in Mexico. I rolled over and reached for the pint of rye.

I was still debating whether to head over the border on foot or not. Of course, if I was going to have a car I knew I'd have to nail one down before the job. I decided hightailing it on foot was the best way. The border was no more than a mile from Mister B's. So to mask the whole thing, I decided to steal a car to pull the job, then ditch it in an alley a block or two from the crossing. I'd spotted a '67 Buick LeSabre not too far from Mister B's when I'd first come to town on the bus. It hadn't been touched all day. Either it didn't run, or the owner was across the border somewhere. There wasn't really any telling when it'd be missed. I actually wanted something smaller and faster, but all the sports jobs and compacts I'd seen looked even more ready for the junkyard than the LeSabre.

I waited till a little past midnight, then walked out of the hotel and down towards Mister B's. When I got to the LeSabre, I found three drunken, arguing Mexes clustered around the car behind it – a Maverick that had had the shit beaten out of it, patched together with a mismatched set of body parts and baling wire.

One of the guys was jabbing a stubby finger in his buddy's fat, drooping gut and chugging a beer with the other hand. The guy who was getting jabbed was pretty schnockered and weaved back and forth in place, trying to keep his balance. The third fellow stood with his hands on his hips, shaking his head disgustedly while he studied them. They were debating the merits of visiting some whore and couldn't come to terms on who was going first.

I casually passed them and bought a newspaper from a battered vending machine. The soberest one, the one who was studying his two buddies, gave me a good once-over as I headed back the way I'd come.

I parked myself against the LeSabre, half-sitting on the hood and perusing the headlines. After a minute or two, the curious one strolled up to me.

"That your car, *señor*?"

"No."

"Oh, I thought you might be the big blonde woman's husband. She park the car, oh, about eight o'clock these morning and walk over the border by herself. *Mucho borracho!*"

I raised my eyebrows. "That sounds like her."

"You know the lady?"

"*Sí.* I was supposed to meet her here an hour ago, but I'm late."

"Hmm, I work there in the shoe shop…" He pointed uncertainly to a storefront a couple of doors away. It was closed up tighter than a drum. "Just closed. I have not seen these lady return, *señor.*"

His two inebriated friends chose my awkward moment to home in on their *compadre*.

"C'mon, Pedro. Why you talking to these gringo? Let us go down to Manuelita's. She is waiting for us."

Pedro gave me one last look, then squinting at his *amigos*, burst out laughing. Throwing his arms around both their shoulders, he shepherded them down the street.

I waited until they were two blocks away, then climbed in the car. It took me only a minute, and I had the two wires I needed stripped and ready to mate. Sparks flew as I touched them together, and the engine coughed, not wanting to turn over. I pumped the gas, and at last she caught.

I made a U-turn, drove past Mister B's and around the block, coming up along the Vasquez Avenue entrance. I parked the car in direct line of vision of the door, then killed it. If I kept the motor running in that neighborhood, I'd return to find no car.

I couldn't see Red, but the beefy mullet-head was at the register flirting with a couple of Mexican whores. I waited till they left, then hopped out, easing off the safety on the .45 I had tucked in my denim jacket's deep pocket.

I didn't have any specific plan. Considering the layout of the place and how little time I'd had for preparation, I figured crashing in was the best idea. If I nonchalantly strolled through those doors, it was a sure thing that Red – if he was there – would spot me for what I was. I needed focused speed and brutality to create the shock and surprise that would give me the advantage.

So, I walked briskly in with my gun out and closed the door behind me.

Red was behind the counter in the chair the mullet-head had been in earlier. He was dozing and didn't realize I was standing right next to him, my eyes boring into his flushed, flabby jowls.

With the whores gone, the kid was now busy stacking cigarette cartons, and he didn't turn around till I was nearly on top of him. When he finally registered the muzzle of the .45 mere inches from his forehead, he gaped at me slack-jawed, unbelieving.

"I want what's in the floor safe."

I don't know what it was, if it was something I was wearing or some vague hint of the Georgia drawl in my voice, but he suddenly regained his confidence. And got lippy.

"No can do there, cowboy."

"Leave off with the satire, fuckface –" I let the end of the automatic rest lightly on the bridge of his nose. " – or I'll give you a new mouth…right between the eyes."

My casual attitude spooked him a little. He didn't start quaking in his boots, just made his face go blank.

"I want that floor safe open. Get your fatass slob of a boss if you have to. I don't really give a fuck what you've gotta do. Just fucking do it."

Keeping the gun snug up against his face, I eased over the counter, then followed him back towards Red. We both paused before the snoring wonder. I kicked Red in the shin, and he started out of slumber, blubbering dreamily. He got all cold and steely-eyed when he recognized me.

"You. I shoulda known."

"Shut the fuck up. The floor safe. Open it!"

"No," he said, real matter-of-factly.

I bashed him across the mouth with the gun barrel, and he fell down on his hands and knees. I waved the gun at the kid.

"You, go lock the front door."

He hesitated.

"Move, goddamn it!"

He jumped, made it to the San Ignacio entrance, slammed the narrow double doors and drew a bolt across them.

"Pull those shades, too."

He did as he was told.

I happened to look back down at Red just in time. Crawling on all fours, he was going for the baseball bat. I kicked his arms out from under him and grabbed the bat myself. He smacked into the grimy, smooth concrete floor face first, making an "oomph" sound as he hit. More blood spurted from his already bleeding mouth.

Meanwhile, the kid was trying to pull a fast one, fumbling to get the doors unbolted so he could get the hell out.

"Don't, kid! I'll fuckin' blow you away!"

He froze.

"C'mon back over here, nice and easy."

He slunk back to the counter with his tail between his legs. I gave him a cold smile.

"Help your pal, Red, there – he's having a slight coordination problem."

The kid bent over and hooked Red under the arms, hoisting him back into the chair. Red was moaning, holding his crooked jaw with both hands.

"You, whoever you are…you'll be dead…dead before…the sun comes up." He stammered it out with trembling fingers over his lips, trying to keep from spitting blood on himself.

I grinned, edging them both closer to the floor safe.

"Only thing is, Red, I won't be anywhere near here when the sun comes up."

I laughed and pushed them down on their knees.

"Open it!" I was starting to get nervous about how long it was taking. Any minute, I knew there'd be customers showing up, getting curious. Right on cue, somebody tried the front door. In the second it took me to look up, the kid went for a sawed-off shotgun under the counter that I hadn't spotted. I smashed him across the front of the head with the .45, and he collapsed in a heap. I rolled him off the safe with one foot. Red barely reacted as the kid flopped limp and fishlike next to him.

The rattling of the doors stopped. I prayed that they wouldn't walk around the block to try the Vasquez Avenue door.

"Hurry up!"

Red had finally gotten the drift that I meant business. He didn't want to get any more beat-up than he was already – let alone killed. His miserable existence had at last become more important to him than the money. He twirled the dial. It only took a couple of seconds, and it was open. I yanked out a large-sized paper bag from under the register and threw it at Red.

"Fill it on up."

This time there was no hesitation. Without the slightest reluctance, Red stuffed thick stacks of twenty, fifty and one hundred dollar bills into the sack.

"It took a while for you to wise up."

He didn't answer, sinking down with his back against a brace of cigarette cartons.

I grabbed a pint of rye, threw it in the sack, then emptied the shells from the shotgun and tossed it all the way across the store.

Red didn't even look after me as I pocketed the .45 and headed for the door.

Chapter 4

Coming out, I ran into a couple of burly guys in seersucker suits and porkpie hats. They started when they saw me.

"We're closed."

The roly-poly one with sweat beading his pudgy face crinkled his eyes. "Closed? Whaddya mean, closed? We're supposed to meet Red here – " he looked at his watch, " – *right now.*"

"Sorry," I said as I walked around the LeSabre and opened the door. "Red wasn't feeling good and 's gone already. The kid's inside closing up."

"Wha –?" It took a few seconds for the strangeness of the whole set-up to register with them. I was already matching up the two ignition wires, pumping the gas as the motor roared to life.

"Hey, who're you?" The other guy, the one with the pencil moustache, was coming up to the passenger side when I rocketed away from the curb.

I looked in the rearview and watched him and his buddy stare at each other. Just before I screeched around the corner heading for the border, I saw the kid stumble out.

I didn't like the two slabs of beef placing me at my mark. I couldn't be any more red-handed if they'd televised it on the evening news. It was a cinch I'd be over the border before either Red or the kid could piece together a coherent sentence between them. And by the time they were able to walk two steps without puking blood, I'd be well on my way across northern Mexico.

But it wouldn't be them coming after me in the next fifteen minutes. It'd be the two gorillas paying the social call and maybe a few more of their friends. A little thing like an international border wouldn't mean anything, especially in Juarez where it only took about a tenth as much to buy up the law.

So I decided not to ditch the LeSabre right away, not to walk over. I'd make as much mileage as I could, then ditch it over there. The whole thing was a stupid cowboy move, so I figured I might as well keep it bigger than life a little longer. Buy some time, then abandon the car in the poorest neighborhood I could find – someplace where it wouldn't stay in one piece for more than five minutes.

I passed right through without incident. The guard barely even looked at me and tiredly waved me through into his sleepy-eyed, hothouse domain. The total opposite of his Anglo counterparts' perversely overprotected fetish of a border – customs boys who will shit bricks of curdled cream if they so much as catch a glint of individuality or the proverbial love-of-life in your woebegone, drug-smuggling, pig's ass of an eye.

Driving across was a shot of raw adrenalin. The smoothness of the brick tread on that potholed thoroughfare was nothing short of miraculous, and a crazy thrill ran through me. I hadn't felt such wild exhilaration since I'd busted Munson's jaw.

There was something else now, too, besides Red's blood drying on my knuckles – the first inkling that, so far, I was getting away with it. I felt a sick twinge of guilt at getting pleasure from pummeling the poor bastard. But it was immediately washed away by his mob connections – and by the fact that any minute a couple of hound dogs trying to pose as human beings would be stumbling along at my heels.

I palmed the wheel, and the Buick swung in a spiraling arc down a darkened alley. Ahead were small, dilapidated houses, some dark, some dotted with the glow of feeble yellow bulbs. At the end, the pavement broke away, dipped off a steep, jagged edge onto uneven dirt. Suddenly there was a pop, then hissing. The front right tire had blown. The car shimmied like a drunken, three-legged dog. I eased it down from the crumbling pavement and pulled the ignition wires. Before getting out, I rolled up the paper bag full of money as tightly as I could, wound a long piece of twine around it to keep it secure and stuffed it under my arm.

A couple of teenage boys sitting and smoking weed on a porch looked up from passing a quart bottle of beer between them. They laughed when they saw I was walking away, leaving a "perfectly good" car in their neighborhood. If I chanced to come back within the half-hour, I'd be sure to find the LeSabre picked clean to the bony chassis, an anonymous metal skeleton.

I figured I'd walk back a block, over two or three paralleling the main street, then cut up to it to try to catch a taxi before Red's buddies could spot me. And after the taxi – what? A taxi might be a good idea. I could get the burly guys doing a real search-and-destroy number on the main drag, which would maybe bring some heat down on them. Which meant I'd only be as safe as the extremely low bribery threshold of whomever would turn out to be my host for the night.

Walking to find that right street, that certain hotel that I could have a good feeling about, put me uptight. For some strange reason I knew the night was not going to be easy. I was impatient to hear that other shoe drop. But it was going to be a long time coming. I would've been a fool to think otherwise.

The pavement started to materialize again. The bricks in the pathetic excuse for a sidewalk became less crumbly. When I came around the corner onto the main drag, I saw how few people were out. Which was bad. And none of the people that were out were white. Which was doubly bad – I'd stick out like a sore thumb.

I stood there at the shadowy mouth of the side street and looked in both directions. There was an anemic but constant flow of traffic, mostly battered, grease-smeared taxis searching in vain for fares. Suddenly, up the street, a bunch of people spilled out of a bar – loudmouth tourists soaked with mescal.

A taxi had already spotted me and was getting ready to hit me up when there was a boisterously noisy surge of asinine behavior from the drunks. The driver's keen ear zeroed in on the sweet music of possible tourist dollars. Bald tires squealed in a u-turn, and the ramshackle jalopy demolished a handcart selling tacos at the opposite curb. The old woman owner went tearing down the street in hot pursuit, but ended up tripping on a beer bottle. Instead of getting up to continue the chase, she just sat there in the pavement with her head in her hands, sobbing. That's when I noticed that every other taxi within a two block vicinity was homing in on the drunks. I guess you'd have to have some kind of built-in radar to do that kind of work. The upshot was that the little old lady was going to get herself squashed flatter than a tortilla by the onslaught of raging automobiles.

An instinct of selflessness suddenly swept over me. I tucked the bag securely under my right arm and foolishly jumped from the shadows to the middle of the street. Not thinking of my own sorry demise, I bent over to pull her up. She then did something totally unexpected, not to mention downright stupid. She resisted and sat right back down again.

"Are you *loco*! You wanna get run over!?"

By this time, though, my question was – how do you call it? – a bit rhetorical since the taxis had already passed us by. So what was I doing there in the middle of the street trying to save somebody who didn't want to be saved, some ancient broad who undoubtedly was completely unaware of any danger at all? Or, if she was, would've probably welcomed it as a convenient exit to her dead-end of a life. I made to leave her there when I felt a tug at my pantleg. There she was, contrite as hell, miming apology with imploring eyes and puffy cheeks. I shook my head and happened to look up again at just the right moment.

Beyond the drunken brigade of tourists surrounded by taxis, I saw it. And I immediately knew it for what it was. There were the burly guys in a gleaming black Continental. I could tell that they hadn't spotted me. They were too busy cursing the traffic jam barring their path.

I whirled to the right, reaching the sidewalk with three giant steps. Behind and to the left of the overturned taco cart was an arcade full of teenage kids making a hell of a racket. And next door, an arched entry to a hotel's narrow stairway. I made a mad dash for the haven that beckoned from beneath sputtering neon.

Once I was through the hotel entrance, I realized the doorway was only for show. It led to an iron staircase that was part of the arcade. Painted yellow arrows that were outlined in Day-Glo orange ascended on the wall next to the steps. I followed, frantic to get away from the brightly lit chamber. The steps spilled onto a flimsy grill of a catwalk overlooking pinball machines, Pac Man and Space Invader games and various vending contraptions.

I wasn't scared, but the noise in the place was confusing me. Everything was running together into one big blur of sound. The cavernous auditorium below was crammed full, mostly with teenage *vatos* and their girlfriends and the unattached women, the whores you'd always be sure to find in a place like that.

All of a sudden, I realized that half the joint had their eyes glued to me. I wasn't playing it smart at all – a gringo fleeing up the stairs. I might as well have left a sign out on the sidewalk for the burly guys.

I tried to calm myself down, take the stairs only two at a time instead of the four I'd been doing when I'd first hit them. Everybody lost interest pretty quickly and went back to being absorbed in their pinball and video games. Bells, horns, mechanical music, robotic jingles repeated over and over as if a record was stuck.

The higher I climbed, the hazier everything got on the arcade floor. Cigarettes and cigars were being consumed at a ferocious pace, and the smoke reminded me of bonfires back home in Mystic. The car club we'd had, we'd all used to get together on cold autumn nights in some forest clearing and torch up a pyre to the full moon.

Just before I got to the top of the stairs, which was the real entrance to the hotel, and the registration counter, I ran into somebody. And what a somebody she was. She was only about five foot five and had a blunt Indian nose that'd been blunted even more by being broken in two different places sometime in the past. In spite of this, she was beautiful. Her huge chocolate eyes bore into me with a pure cold fire that any sweetness, any tenderness or gentleness, had been burnt out of years ago. They were scary eyes. Scary because they saw right through me. I was taken aback, not just from my clumsiness in running into somebody I hadn't noticed, but by the sheer naked power of her will, a will I could see boiling up out of those limpid, razor-sharp pupils. There was a brutal intelligence below the surface that reminded me of Connie.

She thrust herself up against me, nestling one thigh straight home between my legs. She hiked up her velvet lavender dress to let one leg rub along my cock. I could've sworn her knee was a hand, it kneaded my flesh with such supple skill. But she had raised both hands to let down her mane of black hair, a thick tangled mess that fell past her ass.

"You don't look quite so happy, gringo. Elise can fix any trouble."

I was forcing myself to keep cool, but I knew I couldn't have been doing that great a job. She took a bony, sweet-smelling finger and wiped the tip of it across my upper lip.

"You is all hot an' bothered."

I smiled, shook my head in frustration, then took hold of her right, hard muscled arm. I steered her onto the landing and back away from the top of the stairs into a shadowy alcove beside the brightly lit counter.

An ancient phone booth was stuck in the corner. I nodded at it, then her, and I saw I was towering over her since we'd left the steps.

She laughed, "Come now, *señor*, handsome man, we can get a bigger room than that."

We both squeezed in. She was starting to get wise that something was up. "You want to make phone call, *señor*? Why with me?"

"No, honey."

"Well, then, let us get a nice room where you can truly enjoy my beautiful pussy."

Her directness and heavy accent made me laugh. She glared at me.

"No one, an' I mean no one laughs at my pussy! Especially a filthy drunken gringo!"

"This filthy gringo is not laughing at you or your private parts, honey. It's just that your direct approach – "

"I don' got time for the – how you say? – slow build?" She was still pissed but could see that I wasn't making fun of her. She shook her head and started to walk away from me.

"What's your name again?"

That stopped her. Smiling, she turned back to face me. "Elise."

"I like that."

"It don' matter you like or no. My life goes on."

I tucked a twenty dollar bill in the hot dark slit of her ample cleavage, and she became almost sickeningly sweet.

"A couple of my friends are down the block looking for me, but I'm playing a joke on them. I want them to think I already went back across the border without them. So they'll have no choice but to relax and spend *mucho dinero* here."

She didn't believe me at all. I could tell by her cold eyes. Her nipples were already standing out hard as rocks through her dress. I brushed them, then dipped one middle finger between the hot moistness of her breasts, rubbing it back and forth.

"There's more where that came from if you help me."

"More now, *Señor* Rough Hands."

I took another twenty out of my pants pocket and marveled at how wet it was, soaked in sweat. I folded it in two, lengthwise, rolled it to form a tight, coiled ring, then reached into her dress, stretching out the taut fabric and slipping it onto her right nipple. When I took my hand away, it left that part of her dress sticking straight out, and she howled with laughter. "I help with your joke."

"Make sure they believe you. And after they go, meet me in my room. My name's Ray."

"Oh, I make them believe me, *Señor* Ray. In much the same way you make me believe you." Her eyes stabbed me, she gave out with a merciless, forced laugh, and she headed down the stairs.

I made my way through a clump of dirty-smelling Indians in rock 'n roll T-shirts and parked myself at the edge of the check-in counter where I could still watch the main drag's entrance. The drunken men had been watching me and Elise, and unapologetically continued to study my every move as I rented a room from the officious, bald fag behind the desk. While I stuck a twenty in the clerk's rouged, acne-scarred face, I forced an exaggerated smile, then turned my head and made a vertical cutting motion towards the drunks with my left hand, since they were blocking the view of my homegirl. The clerk nervously laughed, tucking a key into the top pocket of my denim jacket. I signed my name on the card he slid under my palm.

A couple of the blotto slobs that were clustered around me were obviously acquainted with Elise, and I'm not sure that it sat well she was consorting with a trashy-looking white boy. Then again, if I hadn't opened my damn fool mouth in their intoxicated presence, my dark hair and eyes, my olive complexion and the shadowy dimness might have painted a different picture.

Elise caught my eye. There was a flurry of awkward movement beyond her from the direction of the street. There they were – the burly motherfuckers. They tried to get past her into the arcade area, but she stopped them with a wild war whoop and outstretched arms. They weren't having any of it, and made with their elbows to shove her aside. But she was a real pro. Not only was she earning her money, she was making a pitch for future employment.

Without warning, the two burly guys became transfixed by the little whore. At first, I couldn't see exactly what she was doing to keep their attention riveted. Two of the Indian guys moved closer to the railing, following my gaze. And then, abruptly, I got an unobstructed view between them. She had the lavender velvet of her skirt hoisted above her thighs, and she didn't have on any panties.

The two Indians signaled their three *amigos* still crowding me at the counter. When all five of them were gathered at the top of the stairs gawking at Elise, they suddenly stopped their slurred, rapid-fire Spanish and drunken laughter. Their silence became a palpably eerie thing.

The burly guy with the moustache sank to his knees on the grimy concrete floor. Elise's hands pushed down on the top of his greasy head, pulling his face close in between her legs. His buddy roared with laughter.

I decided that I'd had enough. I turned into the dingy hall to the left of the counter and headed for the room. I fished the key out of my pocket and groaned as I glimpsed the number 13.

Chapter 5

The number on the door was scrawled off-center at about eye level and looked as if some awkward kid had done it with poster paints. I slipped the key in the lock and gave it a turn. It wouldn't quite give. I leaned into it a bit, and the lock yielded, but the door would only come open a couple of inches because of the uneven floor. I shoved it hard, it banged against the wall, then I was all the way inside.

It was dark. At first, all I had to go by was the fluttering dimness coming in from the grimy window. I squinted and barely made out a small lamp on a night table beside the very narrow double bed. Flipping it on, it only added a meager 25 or so watts of illumination to the drab beige complexion of the room. I sank like a stone onto the sagging mattress and nearly ended up cross-legged on the floor.

Abruptly I remembered the money sack I still had clutched in a vise-grip between my upper arm and side. Letting go, my muscles uncoiled from charley horse tensions, and the sack spilled onto the bare linoleum beneath my feet.

"Goddamn it!"

The half pint of rye skidded out of the paper wrapping and broke against the baseboard, immediately filling the room with heady, distilled fumes.

I picked up the bag, unraveled the crinkled brown paper moist with sweat and pulled a nice fat wad of bills out onto the stained, threadbare bedspread.

There'd been a dramatic dip in the obnoxious noise level the second I'd shut the door, but I hadn't been really conscious of it until then. There was a dull, heavy thud from down the corridor, followed by a light rapping on the wood.

I immediately stuffed the greenbacks into the sack.

"Who's there?"

"Elise…I am alone."

"Come on in." Right when I said it, I realized that I hadn't locked the door. I was starting to feel like a real five-star idiot. It was undoubtedly the strange, sleazy charge of lowdown sex I'd gotten from Elise that was clouding my brain like the thickest of San Francisco fogs. I slipped the .45 out of my belt as she slipped into the room.

"*Madre mia!* It smell like a whiskey factory!"

"Close the door, and lock it."

She laughed and gave me a dirty look over her shoulder while she twisted the latch.

"*Señor* Ray, you did not exactly tell me the whole God's truth."

"How's that?" I could tell she pretty much knew the story, except for the details. I supposed it didn't matter.

"They say when they find you they gonna beat the holy livin' shit outta you. Before they kill you within an inch of your goddamn life. Then they be awfully glad to give me a reward for helping them get their money back. Their money that you stole."

She plopped down on the lumpy mattress practically on top of me, slinging one leg over my knee. She reached out for my gun. "Hmm, that's an awfully nice big one you got there, *Señor* Ray."

"And you did what I told you to do? Do they think I'm miles from here? Like back across the border?"

"They are not so exactly sure one way or another. Once they describe you – "

I was getting pissed even though I knew I should play along with her.

"Goddamn it! When did you have time to listen to any description? What with that ugly-as-sin motherfucker going down on you right in front of all the other sleazeballs out there?"

She ignored me, using a middle finger to probe at the edge of the bag in my lap, and I grabbed her wrist with bone-crushing force.

"Hey, fuck you! Let go, you hurting me!"

I loosened my grip but didn't let go.

"Okay, gringo, you are very righteous. You give me a job

which you pay good money for. I did not tell them you were here. The oily one ask the questions while the other one eat my pussy. The oily one got nasty when he think, no, he know I recognize the description. I push the sex-crazy one away and say, 'Yeah, sure I know him. But he left here fifteen minutes ago.' They both say real funny, because they say it together, 'He's gonna come back, right?' Me, I say, 'How I know? I am not 'is mother!'"

Her chocolate eyes melted back down in the direction of the sack. I slipped my hand into my pocket and pulled out another twenty. When she grabbed at it, I hoisted it high up in the air.

"So, where are they now? Did they leave?"

Her eyes darted up and down between the bill and my rock-steady gaze.

"What if you do not like my answer? You still give me the money anyway?"

I relented, pushed the grubby paper into her grasping palm and nodded. "Since it seems you're telling the truth."

"Oh, sure I am. You kidding, Ray?" She shoved the twenty down her front. "Well, I do hate to tell you this, but since it is the whole God's truth – they checked into a room down the hall. Room 19, I think. I have to go back down there for a little party – "

"Why did you let them check in here!"

She looked at me indignantly. "You son-of-a-bitch! What you think? You tell me they are your friends, no?" She laughed a nasty, cynical laugh. "But as I thought, they tell me who they really are, and you tell me who they really are by this anger in your voice. It makes sense, what they say to me. And this nice, big, fat, oh-so shiny gun of yours." She reached down between my legs as she said the last bit, and she managed to get a rueful smile out of me, even though I was ready to smack her. I pushed her hand away.

"What about this party?"

"I have to go down the hall to entertain them. I no like, I rather stay here with you. You are at least better-looking. I try to – how you say? – put off my girlfriend on them, but they no buy. They say me is who they want. Then they give me these."

She bent over, lifting one foot and slipping off one of her high heels. She plucked something small and green from it, then opened her mouth grossly in a giant O, rotating her long snakelike tongue the total circumference of her nearly black lips as she unfolded a hundred dollar bill. Seeing the high denomination made me break out into a sweat.

"Is not exactly something I want to argue about, eh? No matter how ugly or greasy they are."

I shook my head and looked away from her. She smoothed my cheek with one hand, then the next thing I knew she was up off the bed, fumbling at the locked door. I stared at her.

She cocked her head over her shoulder and smiled slyly. "Do not, worry, Ray. Your secret is safe with me. I know you are good for a little more money, too. But, as I say, do not worry about them. These 'friends' of yours are the kind who would promise me much *dinero*, then, when I have betrayed you, they kill me, too. Besides, Ray, there are some things even I do not sell, no matter how much money is involved." She winked at me, then was gone.

For some strange reason I believed her. The best thing to do, I thought, would probably be just to sit tight and wait for her to come back. It'd probably be a few hours, she'd end up getting rid of them, and they'd go looking for me somewhere else, under some other rock. In the meantime...

I picked up the ancient phone, cradled it in my lap, then shouted into the receiver. Whoever was at the other end – the gay dude at the counter, I think – got the message and promised a bottle of mescal would be in my possession within minutes.

I sat there holding the .45. The money sack tucked between my legs, I bit the nails on my free hand, nails that barely existed they were already so close to the quick. A knock on the door made me jump, but I rapidly regained my composure.

"Yeah?"

"Mescal, *señor*."

"Okay, just a minute." I jacked a bullet into the .45's chamber as noiselessly as I could. Slowly, I turned the knob. The acne-scarred face of the clerk peered nervously around the edge of the splintered, peeling-paint wood. I swung the gun behind my back, simultaneously produced a ten dollar bill with my other hand and exchanged it for the clear glass bottle the clerk was holding out to me as a kind of peace offering.

I smiled. His meek expression dissolved into a lopsided grin.

"*Muchos gracias.*"

I grabbed the bottle and shoved. He stumbled backwards as the door slammed in his face.

I set the sack down on the bed, and the gun and the mescal on the night table. I squatted beside the smelly mattress, pulled back the threadbare bedspread to reveal an equally threadbare sheet. Gingerly,

I lifted the misshapen mass away from the boxspring, then tucked the bag between the two. I yanked up the mescal bottle as I let the mattress fall into place and, with one impatient motion, plopped back against the wall. The flimsy paper seal disintegrated in my fingers as I twisted off the metal cap. Tilting up, bubbling it nice and long, I stuck my tongue against the rim so if the worm headed for my mouth I wouldn't end up swallowing the obscene, bloated thing. Since I couldn't remember the last time I'd eaten, the stuff hit me like a sledgehammer. Before I knew it, I'd stupidly fallen off to sleep.

Chapter 6

When I opened my eyes again, I sat bolt upright, and my head felt as if it was splitting in two.

My gorge rose, and I leaned over the other side, dry heaving over the dirty linoleum. Finally getting my convulsive stomach calmed down, I slowly raised my left wrist close to my struggling-to-focus eyes. The watch showed a good hour and a half had flown by since Elise had left.

I eased off the bed, expending the greatest of effort to keep my head pointed in one direction. The least tilt to one side brought a dizzying spasm of nausea. Miraculously, the .45 was still resting beside the mescal. I slid off the bed and snaked both hands under the mattress. The sack was still in place, too. Hopefully I hadn't screwed myself by falling off to dreamland. Everything seemed to be okay.

I took a palsied grasp of the mescal and upended it once more in the general direction of my throat. I only coughed once, then set it down. I sat there for about thirty seconds, and my head stopped pounding as the alcohol hit. I pounced on the .45, jammed it into my belt and recklessly threw open the door. Right away all the teeth-grinding pandemonium welled up from the arcade. No one was in the hall.

I followed the numbers as best I could – not as easy as you might think since several of them resembled nothing I'd ever seen before – and was careful to make as little noise as possible, probably an unnecessary precaution when you considered the commotion from downstairs.

At last, there it was. Room 19, the formidable bastion of my foes, the burly motherfuckers. I pressed one ear to the door. Nothing – not a peep. I thought maybe the best thing for me to do would be to just confront the bastards, kill them if I had to and wrap up one loose end right from the start. Why not? I looked behind me down the hall as I eased the .45 out of my belt, cocked it and slowly turned the doorknob. I still couldn't hear anything from inside. Maybe they'd finished up with Elise and split already. For the first time, the most obvious answer to why the room seemed unoccupied struck me. When I opened the door the rest of the way, I was totally unprepared for what I found.

Elise was sprawled on her knees in the lap of an overstuffed, coming-apart-at-the-seams easy chair. Her head was twisted around almost behind her at an obscenely unnatural angle. Her eyes were wide-open, staring right at me – but seeing nothing. Then I saw the blood all down her front, spattered in different shades of scarlet and rusty brown across her bare breasts and stomach, and a coagulating black from the jagged wound of a smile that had been slit across her throat.

The full horror of Elise's appearance drove my gaze elsewhere in the room. And that's when I realized two other very quiet, still human figures kept her company. The burly motherfuckers – they were in bed, both dead as a doornail, tucked beneath a baby-blue bedspread now dyed a livid purple from the sickening wave of crimson that had bled from their bodies. Both were naked, their cheap suits piled in awkward heaps on either side of the raggedy mattress. Like Elise, they had had their throats slit.

There was a noise from the bathroom, something that doubly startled me because my poor excuse for accommodations only had a lone sink opposite the bed. I raised the automatic as the door came open and its light went off. Standing framed in the narrow entry was the last person in the world I expected to see: the mullet-head from Mister B's.

He smiled a crooked, mean smile. "Howdy, asshole."
The gashed welt I'd given his forehead at Mister B's was itching, and he scratched at it with the needle sharp tip of a gigantic Bowie knife.

"This is a nice surprise. I thought I was going to have to come looking for you."

"Just done washing off the blood, I take it?"

"You a smart boy, Ray. Hey, don't look so surprised. That's one thing I did get that whore to tell me before she died. Yer name. Me, I'm Eli. I'm Red's son."

Then it rang a really obvious bell. Hadn't the kid with the skateboard told me his name, that the mullet-head was Red's son?

"Where's the dough?" He slowly came towards me.

"You got some balls, Eli. I'm the one with the gun."

"Yeah? Well, I could throw this clean through yer goddamn gizzard and have it out again all nice 'n' wiped before you even pulled the trigger."

I squeezed off a shot that ripped the denim from between his legs and made him stop in his tracks. A thin stream of blood trickled from the graze on his inner thigh.

"Nice lucky shot. Oh, well." He smirked. "I guess we got us a truce for the time bein'. You just better know yer gonna have to kill me to keep me from gettin' that money back. And to keep me from killing you." His mouth widened into a smarmy grin full of crooked, yellow teeth.

I found myself transfixed, staring at his ugly mug while my mind raced for a way out and away from him. He was obviously a psycho, something that made him much more dangerous than twenty of the burly motherfuckers he'd killed. They were just strong-arm schmoes in the business for whatever chump change jokers like Red decided to throw their way. But Eli enjoyed his work. All I had to do was look around the room to figure that out.

"You ever seen so much blood, cowboy?"

I didn't answer him. Instead, I backed up towards Elise, reached out with my free hand and gently shut her mascaraed lids over the glassy pupils.

"Don't tell me you felt anything for that shitass greaser?"

I stared blankly at his scornful face.

"You think yer better than me, don't you? That look on your face..." He laughed. "...You lookin' at me like I'm not even human." Phlegm rattled in his turkey neck as he chortled. "It doesn't pay to be a human. No fun. I'd much rather be an animal."

"You're more than qualified."

He nervously tapped the long thick blade against his leg.

"So, what're we gonna do? Stare each other down the rest of the night?"

I didn't answer, but thought about forcing him out on the landing and having the clerk call the Federales.

"I can read your sorry-ass mind. It won't work. Sure, maybe you can get these stupid fuckin' peons to believe I killed them three, but how're you gonna explain yer little ole bag of money? 'Cause I will tell them about it. Shit, down here in tacoland they're gonna be more interested in American dollars, especially that many American dollars, than three dead bodies and the guy who killed them."

"Maybe so." I brought up something that was puzzling me, even though it fit in with his psycho behavior. "Why'd you kill your Dad's errand boys? Seems he won't take take it too kindly."

I knew the answer before he even opened his mouth.

"Gimmie a break, cowboy. You born yesterday or what? I tell Pop you killed Dom and Sid and got away with all the money. And –"

"Meanwhile, you salt the dough away in some safe, quiet, unsuspected place."

"You are smart."

I thought of killing him right there and then. There were already three other corpses that would soon be starting to stink up the room. Why not a fourth? After all, there wasn't a thing to connect me with the room. But, as much as I rationalized him deserving it and being the safest way out for me, I couldn't do it. Not in cold blood. I felt like a moron. I was optimistic, though, that he'd give me some righteous provocation at any moment.

"Let's go," I motioned him towards the door with the .45.

"You out of yer goddamn mind? Yeah, you are."

That was his cue, and he was right on it. He launched the knife like it was some kind of miniature guided missile. I squeezed the trigger, aiming at the huge blade as it whistled straight for me. The bullet actually hit it, splitting it in two so the bottom half – the point – went spiraling at supersonic speed into one of the burly guy's eyes, while the top half – the hilt with a broken jagged edge protruding from it – ricocheted back towards Eli, embedding itself in his upper right thigh. It was a freak accident, something I wouldn't have been able to duplicate in a million years.

Eli sank down on his ass, his face a mask of blank surprise. He didn't shout or cry, only gave out with a barely discernible whimper. Neither of us said anything for at least thirty seconds. I could still hear the noise downstairs and doubted anyone had heard the shot.

"You fucking dirty rotten yellow son-of-bitch bastard!" He suddenly looked up at me with terror in his eyes, tears rolling down his cheeks. "I'll kill you. You hear me? You stupid worthless Okie!"

I walked over and peered down at him. Without warning, he

had the broken knife out of his thigh and was slashing at my stomach
with it. I kicked it from his hand while I smashed the gun barrel
squarely across the welt I'd given him earlier. He went out like a light.
I didn't wait for him to come to. I knew I hadn't killed him, and it
bothered me. I felt weak because of it. But I couldn't kill him in cold
blood. It was second nature, a reflex.

     I looked around the room for the key and luckily spotted it
right away, lying on the floor in a pool of Elise's blood. I picked it up.
The blood on it was black and sticky as molasses. I had to use some
heavy elbow grease to rub it off, using the bedspread. I left Eli and the
death chamber locked up tighter than a drum.

     Back in my room, everything was as I'd left it. My watch said
I'd only been gone a mere fifteen minutes. That's when I realized I still
hadn't counted the money yet. I knelt down, reached under the
mattress and brought it out. Scattering the contents on the bed next to
me, I started in on it. That's when I realized I'd gotten away with a hell
of a lot more than I bargained on. There were thick clumps of loose
bills as well as four fat stacks bound with paper bands. I could see
that much at a glance. But what I was just noticing now were the
denominations. The clumps had a few twenties, but the primary
numbers were fifties and hundreds. I took hold of the stacks and was
shocked to see nothing smaller than thousand dollar bills. The loose
bills amounted to something in the neighborhood of $15,000. And there
were twenty-five thousand dollar bills in each thin stack. So the entire
haul was around $115,000. I couldn't believe it. With this much, there
was no need for some dope deal. I could head back to Mystic without
any more bullshit, without any more sticking my neck out.

     I crammed the dough back into the frayed, coming-apart sack,
tucked it into my pants next to the automatic and took one more
gluttonous swig from the mescal. No wonder I'd had a hangover after
my nap – the bottle was now only a third full.

     Suddenly an uncontrollable fear welled up inside of me,
making me feel as if I was going to fly apart. Abruptly, the mescal,
rushing like an express train through my raw empty stomach, hit
receptors in my panicky brain so an invisible baseball mitt reached out
into the nightmare sky, catching my soul that some evil smartass was
trying to belt right out of the stadium of my body.

     I killed the bottle, then left the room.

Chapter 7

The noises in the hallway didn't seem quite as loud as a few moments before. The colored lights from the arcade pulsed at the end of the corridor, fighting their way through the smoky haze. I realized for the first time that the walls and floor were curved in a crooked angle towards the counter on the landing.

The group of Indians was gone, and the slight flimsy creature charged with the task of doling out rooms huddled by himself in the shadow of the slotted, numbered key shelves. Not that I'd been around that many dope fiends, but I'd seen a few junkies in my day, and this fellow definitely fit the bill. I could tell he was trying to get as far away from the bright, painful light and excruciating noise as his captive position behind the counter would allow. A sheen of oily sweat coated his entire insubstantial countenance. It made the nervousness and anxiety emanating from his pathetic features into something more. His eyes glowed with apprehension and what seemed like a halo of fear framed the crown of his balding pate.

I tossed the key on the counter. When he made no move to pick it up, I reached for it, leaned over and pushed it into the slot marked 13 that was nearly blocked by his right ear. As the key clinked he jumped and forced his nearly non-existent lips into a quavery grin. I reached down into my pants and fished out another twenty. It crumpled as I crammed it into his soaked shirt pocket. Instead of evaporating, the fear on his face deepened until it creased his smooth cheeks.

The heavy tread of military-issue boots and a shadow falling across my shoulder finally made me understand. As I turned, I thought at first I must've been seeing and hearing things. Then something just below my line of vision caught my attention. I tried to look down as casually as possible so as not to insult the short policeman standing a mere two inches in front of me.

I glanced back at handsome, gave him the sign and started towards the stairs. Something hard and flexible hit me in the stomach. I looked down and saw what I'd expected to see but couldn't quite believe. A leather swagger stick held by the sadistic-looking martinet beside me.

"Just a minute, *señor*. I do not believe I have seen you here before."

"You haven't, Colonel." He was a captain but I thought flattery was the best policy. "But I take it that in one of the tourist capitals of the grand land of Mexico and a border town to boot, it is not particularly unusual to come across strangers."

"I am Captain Emilio Herrera of the Juarez Federal Police." Then his smile displaying two uneven rows of nicotine-stained teeth, disappeared. "Jorge," he gestured over his shoulder with a gloved thumb at the androgynous hophead, "made a telephone call. *Señorita* Moreno had asked him to call me because she was – how would you say? – concerned. She wanted to make sure that nothing happened to her."

I knew he had to mean Elise. "*Señorita* Moreno?"

"*Si, si,* probably you know her." He turned to sweaty Jorge, who looked at me with trepidation. Jorge finally nodded, and the captain swiveled his strange little head back up to face me. "She goes by her Christian name, Elise."

I nodded, "*Si,* Colonel, but she decided that she liked two other gentlemen better. She went off with them an hour or so ago."

El Capitan stiffly turned his whole torso this time.

Jorge shifted from one spastic foot to the other. "Is true, my captain. Two other gringos. In room 19."

Suddenly, there was a commotion from the hallway. A bellowing swell of feline, feminine yet barely human screams and shouts from Eli, my psychotic nemesis. Captain Herrera lost interest in me and moved with astonishing speed. Needless to say I took advantage of his preoccupation to make my exit. But not before relieving Jorge of the obvious burden my additional twenty dollar bill was causing him. He gave out a cry that reminded me of a possum catching its tail in my little cousin Mary Lou's tricycle spokes.

"That's for making the telephone call, Georgie."

I vaulted down the stairs and out into the street.

Chapter 8

I hit the sidewalk at as brisk a pace as possible without running. My appearance would cause enough comment as it was. The population of the boulevard had increased appreciably, and at least a third of the new traffic were gringos. Still, a running, obviously transient white man would draw attention. Even though I was sure the locals weren't given to cooperating with the police, I knew that if I fled I would be remembered.

Just ahead of me, on the same side of the street, I noticed a battered '77 Chevrolet masquerading as a police car trying to ease itself out of the parking space. It'd been wedged in tight by a stupendously ugly yellow stepvan. That the driver of a civilian truck had had the balls to block in a vehicle driven by a no doubt grouchy *Federale* was a mystery I had no time to contemplate. At that inopportune moment, Captain Herrera materialized from the mouth of the alley directly ahead of me. He was no more than six or seven yards away, and the only reason he didn't spot me immediately was due to his heading in the opposite direction.

I spun around only to be greeted by the sight of two policemen hustling Eli out of the arcade/hotel entrance. The clothes of all three men were in tatters, a flurry of bloody, torn fabric blurring in the frantic motion of limbs pistoning and pummeling each other. Eli wasn't going along peaceably, to say the least. Luckily for me there was so much confused excitement from the influx of rubberneckers, I went unnoticed. As quickly and casually as possible I made my way to the back of the stepvan, swung open the rear doors and climbed into the waiting darkness.

A rancidly sweet odor of decay all but overpowered me. It was like being in a butcher shop in a tropical climate a few days after refrigeration had broken down. It was so bad it made me forget nearly everything else, that I was on the run and that there was a threat right outside. I tried to make out my surroundings in the blackness and found my eyes gradually growing accustomed to the van's interior. There were two shelves on either side hanging from the walls like bunks. Except, of course, they weren't. I thought for a second that it might be an ambulance. Then I realized there wasn't any kind of medical equipment inside. And the smell – yeah, that's what it was all right. A meat wagon – from the morgue. Captain Herrera somehow knew he was going to need it. Which didn't make sense.

I knew why it was there. Eli's handiwork. It had to be that. Any minute the corpses of Elise and the two burly motherfuckers were going join me in the darkness. And if I didn't find some nook or cranny to hide in, I'd be joining them in a much more permanent style than I had in mind.

As if on cue, I heard a commotion from the sidewalk. Somebody banged against the driver's side door. Then it was open. The somebody settled into the driver's seat, whistling a happy-go-lucky Mex tune I didn't recognize and firing up the engine. The carburetor coughed noisily, threatening to die a tubercular death. The fellow knew his beast, though, and nursed it along with his foot on the accelerator. Suddenly, he rammed the shift into first, there was a deafening grinding like King Kong's fingernails along a skyscraper blackboard, and we lurched away from the curb.

I figured he was pulling up even with the hotel entrance so they wouldn't have to haul the stiffs so far. His lead foot descended on the brake pedal. I was thrown forward onto the greasy floor and for the first time noticed the pile of dirty rags beneath the bottom bunkshelf on my left. It looked big enough to give me adequate cover. A rattling of the back door handle startled me so I dove straight into the evil-smelling scraps of cloth. By the time the morgue boys had it open and were loading my late acquaintances, I was hidden by the rags – two malodorous sheets that had been torn in half. Four polyester pieces caked with cracked, greasy brown blood covered me from head-to-toe.

Even breathing through my mouth I could still smell the nauseating stench of death. It welled up around me, a liquid mass of obscene, claustrophobic mortification. I prayed that I wouldn't start retching. Already convulsions were reverberating in my stomach, trying to escape up into my esophagus, trying to strangle me, find release.

A machine-gun banter of slurred Spanish filled the van as two drunken attendants stumbled against the shelves with their cargo. Apparently they loaded the two burly mothers in first, leaving Elise for last. As they placed her carelessly on the bunk directly above me, I heard a familiar voice. It was Captain Herrera standing in the gutter outside. He barked in a high-pitched nasal whine that made him sound even sillier than he had been speaking English.

Suddenly there was an eruption of gunfire from in front of the stepvan. Herrera got in one last growl of angry frustration and slammed the back doors. I could hear the two attendants mumble incoherently, frightened. Then one of them was at the wheel again, trying to start the engine. The stepvan lurched as he threw it hurriedly into gear and stepped on the gas.

There was the explosion of another shot, this one's bullet ripping through the truck's metal skin as we passed the gun battle. It tore into Elise's dead flesh, making a muffled thump. The panicked driver rammed the truck into high gear, hurtling us over bumps and potholes. He negotiated an abrupt left turn. The burly mother positioned over Elise and I flopped and thudded heavily onto the vibrating floor. I pulled the stinking piece of sheet away from my head just in time to have Elise's lifeless hand thwack me in the face. An involuntary shiver spasmed my shoulders together, and a chill raised the hackles on my neck. It was the coldness of her rather than the being startled. I jumped up. Elise was still covered by her sheet. But my burly friend who was sprawled on the floor stared at me with glassy eyes.

"Madre mia!"

I locked stares with the attendant in the passenger seat. Funny, I couldn't think of anything but that he sounded Italian, not Spanish. Curious about his *amigo's* outburst, the other one craned his neck in a nearly impossible contortion. Immediately a lead foot again descended onto the brake pedal, and all of us, including our deceased companions, lunged forward.

I could see through the bug-flecked windshield that we'd come to a stop in the middle of a darkened, comparatively quieter neighborhood. Realizing that neither of the attendants were armed, I casually drew my .45 and approached the front of the deathwagon.

Both sets of eyes widened in consternation. I'd all but forgotten my advantage, even though it'd been poking me uncomfortably in the groin ever since I'd assumed a horizontal position beneath the late Elise.

For the life of me I couldn't think of the Spanish words for "train station." Noticing my hesitation, the driver spoke up.

"Don't worry, *señor*, I speak English if that is your concern." Then he laughed, and there was a sweaty quavering in his voice and the smell of anxious farts.

I realized if I had them drop me off at the train station I'd have to kill them. And even then the stepvan would still be in the proximity of the station, so it'd be more than obvious how I'd skipped town. Any way I looked at it, I was screwed.

My smiling, oh so cooperative driver stamped on the gas and sent us flying. The momentum threw me forwards into the dash and windshield, the gun smashing the safety glass into a dented spiderweb of transparent pebbles.

The passenger attendant, whom I now had my back to, grabbed my right wrist and with his other hand tugged on my jacket collar with all his might. I caught sight of the driver's frightened face as I flew backwards. He was trying to steer the truck to an open space at the curb without crashing into any parked cars and, at the same time, avoid the barrel of the .45. Unfortunately his idiot partner had me swinging back and forth in such a way that he was perpetually in my line of fire. They both shouted in panicky bursts of Spanish while I tried to mash my heel down on my assailant's toes. He sprang, letting go of my collar but using his forward motion to snare my throat in the crook of his arm. He was in good shape, and his muscled limb was a vise around my neck. His grip tightened as the stepvan came to a stop, and I felt myself starting to pass out. A grey screen was gradually slipping across my vision. One of the last things I saw was the driver coming at me with a knife he'd drawn from his belt. With one last effort I stomped down on my strangler's foot, and he howled in pain. I simultaneously swung him around so the .45 again pointed at the driver. Nearly hysterical, he let go of the steering wheel and plunged the knife straight for my breast-bone. I ground my heel as hard as I could into the toes of the guy choking me. His larynx-crushing grip abruptly relaxed but his other hand tightened on my gun. His fingers snaking around mine yanked the trigger in a spasmodic fit. Three shots erupted point blank, and the driver's face exploded in a blossom of spiraling viscera, eyeball and splintered cheekbone. Still, his dagger flew forward, flying in an arc upwards as the bullets sent the rest of him reeling backwards onto the seat. The blade caught me below the belt. If there had been the original full force of his blow behind it, I would have been castrated. As it was the sharp steel ripped the front of my jeans and the paper bag full of money.

My other attacker had stopped at the concussion of the shots. His bloodlust frenzy had subsided into shocked horror at the sight of his deceased, mutilated *compadre*. I spun around to cover him. At first, he didn't react, his stare riveted in morbid fascination. Without warning he came out of his momentary stupor and, growling like some hurt, wild beast, came flying at me. I tripped as I stepped backwards and pulled the trigger, immediately spotting a neat, round red hole appear in the middle of his forehead. He tottered for a fraction of a second, then plummeted to his left, landing full across the one burly mofo still beneath the gross sheet.

I fell into a sitting position on the edge of the bunk where Elise's body lay. The deathwagon's smell mixed with the rush of blood and adrenaline bent me over, my head between my legs, and I puked my guts out.

Chapter 9

I found myself stumbling along an unlighted, partly paved, partly dirt street. At first I couldn't remember where I'd left the stepvan or the direction in which I'd set out.

There was the faint brightening of the slum skyline to the east, like someone had placed a bulb of extremely low wattage beneath the surface of greasy, opaque dishwater. At last the night of death and horror was over.

Remembering, I looked down at myself. My shirt and jacket were streaked with blood. It wasn't as noticeable on my jeans. Everything rushed back over me in a flood of. . . dreams. Unreal nightmares full of recrimination for my own sad self. And not just recrimination, but horrid imaginings of complicity in the sado-manboy's brothel slaughter.

I imagined what it was like to slit the burly motherfuckers' fire-hydrant excuses for throats. Then I could see Elise's bare brown flesh opening up against the whisper of Eli's knife, feel her skin peeling back like the blossoming flower petal of blood that it was, and I collapsed to my knees on the crumbling brick that made up the sidewalk. My gut heaved, and I felt my esophagus, already raw from my last bout of vomiting, constrict in a nauseous frenzy. There was nothing left to bring up.

When I raised my head, I saw an old man in a torn undershirt and blue denim overalls so greasy they were a slick ashen black. He was standing beside a rickety fence in front of a ramshackle plywood house. Silent, stoicly ambivalent, he eyed me over his loosely-packed, handrolled cigarette. A wreath of smoke went up around his head, blotting out his glassy stare. When I looked away from him, he turned and walked back into his hut.

All of a sudden, I felt acute anxiety for my material welfare and grabbed inside my shirt to see if my paper bag of money was still there. It was, tucked in its knife-split brown bag. I could see the green edge of a wad of fifties and pushed it deep down again against my aching groin. I wanted to button up my shirt, but the bottom buttons where it counted most were gone, torn away from the knife in the meat wagon. My .45 was still where I'd tucked it, jammed behind me in my waistband, digging into the small of my back.

I needed to get to the train station. From there, I'd head south in an eastern diagonal, stop once I felt I'd run far enough, then start back northeast, probably to Matamoros. I'd cross the border to Brownsville, then take another train. If I felt at all uncomfortable – like maybe somebody's face looking a bit too familiar – then I could always change in New Orleans. Hopefully sooner than later I'd roll into Mystic and Connie Eustace's arms. The last time I'd called her was right before I'd started thumbing out of Coronado. She hadn't been home, but Mama swore she'd pass along my message.

Mama, crazy as ever. Crazy as a fox. She was working some kind of money-laundering scam fronted by a mail-order country records business out of a phony Nashville address. Lucky Fordyce was the "artist," a fifty-year old good-natured has-been who, for some reason, was still able to sell records, cassettes, CDs, whatever from TV ads but couldn't chart worth shit. His last real hit was in '79, something that had gotten to number 20 in the country charts. He'd had one in the low 40s in 1984. But back all through the sixties he'd had a decent string of heart-tuggers and honky tonk smashes that had made him a millionaire several times over. Of course, being a country star, that had meant it was nearly all gone by the end of the seventies. Now he lived in Mystic. When his manager had concocted the mail-order scheme, it had been to try to make back some portion of the money he'd advanced to Lucky on the downhill slide. Lucky had known Mama and brought her in to help run the phone operation part, so she had to deal with all the 800-number bullshit. And it served as a money-laundry conduit for Mama's, Lucky's and the manager's drug dealing.

I looked up and found myself staring into a dirty pane of glass. It was an abandoned building a block from the train station. I could barely make out my reflection. It cut off my head, but seeing from the shoulders down reminded me of my gory appearance. I stripped off my jacket, turned the denim inside out and was relieved to see that the brownish scarlet had barely soaked through. I jammed the paper money bag down into the other side of my crotch, away from the ragged, two-inch slit the knife had made and, at the same time, plucked several twenties. I stuffed them into my right pocket while impatiently ripping away the two remaining buttons on my shirt. The blood spray from my assailants had created an abstract oblong down the front where my jacket had been open. There was no question; it was hopelessly ruined.

A train whistle blew, and I caught myself staring, hypnotized by the dull brown-red reflection. Across an assortment of rubbish-strewn vacant lots I could see a train sitting in the station, obviously readying to pull out – perhaps in a matter of minutes. I yanked at the seamy cloth, furious at myself for spacing out when I needed to remain alert to remain alive. Balling up the shirt, I threw it on top of the roof of the one-story building, then climbed into my inside-out jacket.

As I ran among the foul-smelling heaps and tangles of garbage on the lot, I became aware of the stickiness inside the denim and an involuntary spasm of chills shivered through me. I made a silent prayer that none of my deceased opponents had the AIDS.

Rounding the corner of the station house, I came up against a crowd of sluggish people, all engaged in either embarking, disembarking or seeing off family or friends. The intolerably bright morning sunlight on the platform made me acutely aware of the sudden upswing in temperature. The painfully evident torpor of every single person in sight made the sun so much hotter, the air so much muggier, I felt an abrupt faintness. I was dimly aware of a tangle of thoughts, that I mustn't hesitate and make myself a target, that the police were undoubtedly watching the station – especially if the psycho fuckface had given them the slip, that only twenty minutes ago it was no more than sixty degrees, that in the time it would take to buy my ticket I could miss the train – if it even was the right one – it did seem to be headed in the right direction.

Then, the shouts and laughter in Spanish brought me around. On the far end of the platform was one lone *Federale* doing his thing. He looked tired, unwashed and irritable, too.

I spotted the ticket window to my right out of the corner of my eye. Keeping the cop in sight the whole time, I casually but quickly walked over to the hole in the wall. When I finally brought my anxious stare away from my unawares target, I could tell there was something wrong right off. The ancient, prune-faced clerk's eyes were huge black olives with a very faint outline of pinkish white around them. He was glaring at me with such a combination of surprise, horror and fear, I thought for a moment that he somehow recognized me. Of course, that was impossible.

"*Bue–buen–buen–buenos d–d–dias, señor.*" His stutter was so exaggerated, I nearly began laughing. Somehow I kept it under control and acted as if there was nothing wrong.

"I'd like a ticket."

"A ticket?"

"Yes, a ticket. You do sell tickets at this window, don't you?"

"*Si, si* – I'm sorry. A– a–ticket to–to where, *señor*?"

"Just give me one to the end of the line. I'm not sure exactly where I'm going."

"That is a rather – how do you say? – ex–p–p–pensive way of doing th–th–things, my friend. No?"

"No. Not for me. It's worth it. Then I can just get off where and when I feel like it."

He made an almost audible gulp, but proceeded to scribble on his ticket pad before him. All the while he continued to glance up at me, as if my face held some fascination or some answer to a puzzle that had long been confounding him. Then he tore it off.

"How much in American money?"

He glanced down at a yellowed, dog-eared page taped and peeling next to his ticket pad. "Thirty-eight dollars, señor."

I reached down into my pocket, glancing over my shoulder to where the cop had been standing, then back to the clerk. The *Federale* was nowhere in sight. I placed two twenty dollar bills on the clerk's ticket pad and took the ticket gently from his grasp with my other hand.

"*Gracias.*"

He said nothing. I turned and walked towards the train. I purposely headed for the last car. Fortunately it coincided with the least amount of people, at least on the platform.

Chapter 10

Once I stepped up into the car I realized it was a totally different story. It was jampacked to the suffocating gills. All the more reason for me to wonder why, out of all these folks, I should be the one to attract attention. I couldn't understand why people were looking at me. Upturned faces peered from lazy positions on wooden benches strung along each side. Those that weren't looking were nudged by companions or complete strangers until everyone was staring in fearful apprehension.

I made my way, stumbling over torn leather satchels, bursting straw bags, soiled cloth bundles and the occasional chicken, to the head. It was located at the opposite end of the car, so I had to run the gauntlet. Scared and confused, people inched back and away, trying to keep from letting me touch any part of them. Finally, after what seemed like an interminable stretch, I came to my destination. The *hombres'* room door was quite a bit shabbier than that of the *mujeres*. At least their unpainted, splintered plywood on hinges was fully intact. The door I pushed open with a rusty squeak had several holes inches from its bottom, right where you would plant a kick once frayed patience and a bladder filled beyond capacity had reached the bursting point.

The splintered wood scraping along the filthy floor as I pulled it closed kept me from noticing that I had company behind a flimsy curtain. Just as I was about to peer behind the foul cloth, I caught sight of my face in the smeary mirror. It was hard to believe I'd overlooked something quite as melodramatic, not to mention incriminating, as a face covered with blood. Somehow, though, I had.

Now I understood the ticketseller's consternation, my fellow passengers' rapt and horrified fascination. There were no towels – cloth, paper or otherwise – so I stripped off my inside-out denim jacket. Finding a relatively clean patch under the right armpit, I wetted the fabric in the sink and applied it to my forehead and rubbed. The thick ichor of slippery congealing death spread beneath the pressure. I brought the jacket down and saw in the pathetic excuse for a mirror – since the sticky blackish-red was nearly dry – that all that I had accomplished was to smear the mess further down both temples. It now blended with the auburn film that coated both cheeks to a slightly lesser degree. I sighed and felt suddenly faint at the stinking closeness, the heat of the microscopic compartment. The low sink that barely reached my thighs was a filthy basin covered with black grease. Two flies buzzed lethargically above it.

I hesitated to use more water for fear of ingesting any of it. I had a phobia of dysentery that bordered on the absurd. After a moment's hesitation I overcame it. Again I rotated the creaking knob on the one rusty spigot and dabbed the denim with the paltry trickle. There was a rustling from behind the flimsy curtain that hid the toilet. Every muscle in my body involuntarily tensed as I rubbed again at the congealed blood. I cocked my head to one side and was able to see a bulky shadow moving in the unlit alcove. There was an intense groan. I glanced down beneath the curtain. A pair of well-dressed knees rested on the disgusting floor before a pair of muddy cowboy boots.

I looked back into the mirror and found that I was finally starting to make some headway in cleaning my face. I bent over and scooped up a handful of water, splashing it across my brow. I clasped the other end of the jacket where I spotted another comparatively clean patch, and dried the wet spots as quickly as I could. Satisfying myself that I was as presentable as possible under the circumstances, I slipped the jacket on again. Almost immediately there came another louder groan from behind the curtain and a hoarse whisper, "Jack. . . Jack!"

I made like I was going to leave the compartment, pressing myself against the vibrating wall where my legs would not be visible beneath the curtain, and then I pried open and closed the splintered bit of plywood.

"Oooh, I thought he'd never leave – hmm, does that feel good, Jack?"

I leaned over and caught sight of a close-cropped thatch of piss-colored straw bobbing before a pale groin. It moved slightly to the right and another pale expanse of skin came into view. There, on the thigh of the fellow receiving this queer bit of affection, was a nasty, unbandaged wound. No, I told myself, it couldn't possibly be. Very carefully, I bent over, raising my gaze as I did so. Eli's ugly pig eyes tilted themselves up from the site of pleasure and looked into mine.

"Harry, we got company."

"What –?" The word came with difficulty from a mouth filled with the psycho kid's unhealthy flesh. Harry shot to his feet as if from a gun, and Eli's huge knobby hard-on stood at attention for but a brief instant before wilting in the fresh air.

"If it isn't the Okie from Mystic." Eli, careful not to brush the scabbed-over gash on his thigh where the broken knife had intruded, pulled up his pants. Harry indignantly threw back the drape of rotten cloth.

"Jack?" I said the name with incredulity.

Eli looked from me to Harry, then back again. "Yeah, that's my name, Ray. Don't fuckin' wear it out. This is my – friend, Harry Aaronson. Harry, this is Ray."

Harry looked about as uncomfortable as he could possibly look. So much sweat was rolling down the expanse of his narrow Neanderthal forehead he had to swipe at it every few seconds with the gabardine sleeve of his charcoal grey leisure suit. There was something about the nervousness of his squinty eyes that made me feel, impossible as it seemed, recognized. "Who–who–the–hell is–is–is this, Jack!"

"Why, Harry, yer not gonna believe it, but this is the friend o' mine I was tellin' ya about. The one I was lookin' for. You know, the one with the connection for all the coke and smack in Agua Caliente."

It was my turn to look uncomfortable. The wheels and cogs were turning at terrific speed inside Eli's warped skull. I watched Harry as his fat tongue, fresh from Eli, lolled out from between jagged teeth and licked his non-existent lips.

"Ray, Harry's a DEA field agent."

Harry's tongue darted back in, and his eyes spit fire at Eli.

"Jack, what the hell're you saying." He looked at me, embarrassed by what was obviously the truth. "Ray? Is that your name? Jack, here's just being funny. Me a DEA agent? That's rich! Ha, ha, ha! Jack, that joke's in rather poor taste."

Without missing a beat, Eli reached into Harry's sweat-soaked polyester jacket and produced a cellophane envelope of Polaroids. Harry's right fist of mottled corpse flesh automatically made a grab for the private treasure, but Eli was too fast, hoisting them playfully over his own head. Harry was a couple of inches shorter so had to stand on tippy-toe then jump each time he made a stab at retrieving the photos. Eli's cruel, gap-toothed grin slowly dissolved into gritted teeth as he turned his inhuman pig-eye stare from Harry to me. Harry suddenly gave up, out of breath and flushed from the exertion and abominable heat. He sank against the crusty, fly-specked pane of grease.

Regaining his composure slightly, he mopped at his skull with a rose-colored handkerchief. He refused to look at either Eli or me, instead pretending to study the onrushing landscape as best he could through the pathetic excuse for a window.

Eli waved the cellophane packet back and forth over his head, then slowly lowered it. He reached out to me, and I instinctively backed away.

Suddenly someone tried to open the frail plywood door.

Eli erupted with a violent kick to the already splintered surface, *"Occupado! Chingas tu madre!"*

Someone on the other side angrily slammed their own foot into the partition. But then from the sound of retreating footsteps, it was obvious whomever needed use of the facilities was unwilling to confront a possibly homicidal maniac.

I turned my gaze away from the door to find Eli already glaring at me with his demonic grin. "Ray, don't be scared. I'm not going to kill you. At least for a while."

"Oh, yeah? What could possibly have changed that coiled snake you call your mind?"

He held forth the cellophane packet of Polaroids by way of answer. I just stared at the transparent plastic rectangle suspended between his thumb and forefinger, unable to make out anything because the picture sides were facing the floor.

"What's a'matter, Ray? Ain't curiosity gettin' the better of you?"

Harry lunged forward from his place at the window, making a grab for his property. I was startled at how easily Eli handled the man, using one leg expertly in an almost kung fu move to swipe Harry's own two spindly pegs out from under him. He crashed face-first on the septic floor. Eli didn't say anything, he didn't even give out his usual sadistic chortle of a laugh. He just kept his eyes burning into mine.

I snatched the envelope away from him, turned it over and withdrew what appeared to be six photos. I couldn't believe my eyes. Mama's picture – her on the telephone obviously in the mail-order office – was right on top. Down in the corner on the shiny white bottom border was scrawled in a barely legible hand – because the ballpoint skipped on the smooth surface – the date: *February 24, 1987*. Over a month ago.

"Your mama's one good-looking woman. Considering her age and all."

I looked up at Eli, still dumbfounded.

"Hey, Ray, close your mouth. A fly might land in it. Especially in this outhouse." He looked down with a disgusted grimace as agent Harry picked himself off the vibrating floor of filth then, folding his arms, leaned against the wall. He glared at me from beneath his hooded heavy brows.

Eli acted as if he wasn't there. "Go ahead, Ray, take a gander at the rest of the snaps. You nearly got the start of a family scrapbook there."

I placed Mama's Polaroid on the bottom of the six and looked at the next. It was Lucky Fordyce smoking a joint with what was probably some secretary – she had her rear to the camera – out in the backyard of what looked like Mama's place. The huge cypress I'd played and climbed on as a kid was in the background. So, too, was Lucky's old '56 Oldsmobile that'd taken a shit in 1980 and had been sitting there rusting away next to the cypress ever since.

"Jack?" Harry's voice was weak, scared. Neither Eli nor I looked over at him. "Jack, you know those pictures are government property. They're also classified. No one's supposed to see them or know about them, especially someone who –"

My head pivoting in his direction shut him up.

"His name's not Jack, it's Eli." I didn't like the feeling that was mushrooming in my lower guts. "Especially someone who what, Harry?"

Harry wouldn't answer.

"See, Harry, you've got Ray all upset now. Ray's someone you do not want to get upset. He's almost as bad as me." He gave me a scornful look. "Ray, Ray, Ray. You're so naïve. Harry knows that Eli's my real name. He's just observing DEA protocol. Trying not to blow my cover. Aren't you, Harry?"

Harry wouldn't even look at me, instead pleading silently with his eyes for Eli to somehow get him off the hook. I couldn't believe a Federal agent could be so gutless. I'd met a couple in Coronado when

I was still in the Navy, and neither one of them, however unreasonable and hardheaded, had been like this.

"Ray, check out the rest of the pix. You'll answer part of the question."

The way he said it made a chill run down my spine. And in that claustrophobic, foul-smelling heat the chill made me break into an icy sweat. I looked at the next one. There were three people whom I didn't immediately recognize. Then once again the shock set in. It was taken from the standpoint of someone standing at the bottom of a huge king-size bed with white satin sheets. In the foreground, sitting on the edge in a deep maroon silk robe, was the stunningly gorgeous Janine Hickock – I knew it was Janine, even though she had an identical twin, because of her sullen, intelligent expression. I could also just make out the black beauty spot on the exquisite chocolate flesh of her high-boned right cheek. A beauty spot I remember brushing my lips against the one time she and I had been intimate when I was just out of high school – the only time I'd been unfaithful to Connie Eustace.

Behind her on the bed – the scene Janine was obviously trying to ignore – the pain and anger and humiliation in her eyes said so – was her twin, Jeannie, kneeling on a giant pillow beneath the ivory headboard, naked as a jaybird. Her huge magnificent breasts seemed poised to bury the bald skull of Mystic's illustrious mayor, J. Calden Jimsen, between them. He was nude, too, except for black bikini briefs and a pair of garters holding up his socks. My heart went out to Janine. But then I remembered there were still three more pictures.

The next had been taken outdoors at night, and it was the only one that was not a Polaroid. It was a small, glossy color print. I couldn't quite make it out at first. I held it closer. The three figures were shadowy, crowded around something on the uneven, weed-choked ground with the cypress tree behind them. Then I recognized two out of three of them – Lucky Fordyce and Mama. I abruptly realized what they were holding – shovels. And they were standing over a grave. The second and third pictures hadn't had dates. But this one was marked by the same shaky hand trying to wield a skipping ballpoint. It looked like *March 10, 1986*. I gave up trying to make out who the other person in the picture was. The top of his – or her? – head was almost completely cut off, and shadows and swirling mist obscured what was left of their face.

I went to the next one and nearly dropped the whole bunch. It was me. Taken at Mr. B's, it showed me holding a gun on Red, pointing it less than an inch from between his eyes. I looked up at Eli. His smile was ghastly, hideous, like some mad dog. Eli laughed, as if he knew what I was thinking.

"I know you think the next picture couldn't be any worse – "

I flipped the last Polaroid over. Suddenly a crimson haze formed around it as I realized what it was – my peripheral vision went into a tunnel. Red's bloody corpse, his face half-blown away, lay there on top of the floor safe and a blood-covered carton of Marlboros.

"You shouldn't've done it, Ray. Why do you think I'm so obsessed with sticking to you? After you killed my father."

I could barely speak. He must have done it himself, right as I ran into the burly mofos outside the store. He had the time. I just couldn't remember hearing any gunshots. Then again, maybe he'd done it after the burly guys left, and that's why he had killed them. They had gone in the joint before following me and knew Red hadn't been shot. The smile on Eli's animal face testified to how much he'd hated his father.

"You son-of-a-bitch! You fucked up one thing though. The bullets will never match. I didn't fire my gun in the store – in fact, I didn't fire it at all until I was in the Juarez whorehouse."

His laugh turned into a self-righteous, pitying smile.

"Ray, you are one naïve guy. Do you think, after receiving an eyewitness report from me, Red's son, that any of Red's pals are gonna turn you over to the cops for a ballistics test? My word is golden. Besides, Harry here already considers you a suspected liaison to your mother's money-laundering, prostitution and drug-dealing operations in Mystic. Yeah, drugs and whores. Don't act like you don't know where the dough comes from. Not Lucky Fordyce's shitty records." He paused. "You're undoubtedly asking yourself the reason why Harry has all these pictures."

I shook my head and leaned back against the wobbly sink.

"Just customary DEA surveillance photos."

I felt as if my feet were already encased in a cement slab, and Harry and Eli were just waiting for the proper moment to throw me off some bridge into the deepest, coldest part of the Mississippi.

"Oh, Ray, I forgot one. I snuck this out of Harry's jacket when he was, shall we say, 'occupied' earlier." Eli fumbled in his shirt pocket as Harry's face flushed a shade so purple I thought he might be on the verge of a coronary. "I always like to save the best for last." The tone in his voice made me involuntarily shudder.

He handed the last, dog-eared Polaroid to me, face-down.

When I turned it over the shock of what and who it was and

what they were doing made me unable to register it as being real.
Even after thirty seconds or so, I still had trouble admitting to myself
it was her. But there was the fucked-up ballpoint scrawl: *CONNIE
EUSTACE MCQUEEN WITH UNKNOWN SUBJECT, December 23,
1985.* My gorge rose and tears flooded my eyes. It wasn't like Connie
and I were any saints, but we'd both been faithful to each other for 99%
of our time together – not because we had to but because we'd both
wanted to. We'd even done something silly – ironically enough
Connie had suggested it – a blood brother/sister pact not to have sex
with anyone else.

And there she was – it was definitely Connie Eustace, her
beautiful black hair, her splendid quarter Cherokee cheekbones
hollowed even more as she sucked some pale white redneck's cock dry.

Chapter 11

What kind of shit was that? What kind of poison was suddenly welling up inside me, that made me want to die, hope to die, but would keep me alive with the seething? An icy flood raced through me. The only thing I could think was that Connie had been drunk.

Suddenly I wasn't in that foul-smelling compartment with the Fed and the psycho.

But I could see Connie as clearly as if she were right in front of me. I bent down over her. She was stretched horizontally across our bed upside down, wrapped in white sheets, her head pointed between my legs. I raised her up, and our lips came together. As always, that fraction of a second before touching her mouth, I could feel a magnetic pull, a hunger that had taken hold of her, too, and there we were devouring each other in a kiss. I slid my hand beneath the sheet that came up to the hollow of her throat, my palm sloping up the heavy, at-rest-roundness of her right breast. The nipple was hard, sticking up to keep my fingers from moving any further. She reached up her left hand to hold onto the back of my neck, snaked her right hand between my legs. Even through my jeans I could feel the rock-hard ropes of veins and tendons below her knuckles. I sighed as she turned it round cupping my hardness with her gentle iron grip. I reached down, smoothing her stomach, the barely visible outline of hair that traced a line from navel to pussy. Then I was running my hand through the silkiness until two fingers discovered the slippery wetness. The sheet was down around her knees, and I was licking her lower lips.

"Hey, sport, move!" Eli's voice was sneeringly petulant. He wagged his head in Harry's direction. The agent was trying to get by me and out the door. Thinking he was tricky, he darted his hand out to grab the obscene Connie photo that was still crumpled loosely in my fist. But Eli beat him to it. Their kindergarten game of one-upmanship was sickening.

Eli, with an exaggerated flourish, smoothed the photo using the graffiti-smeared wall for support.

Harry made with a hissing, melodramatic intake of breath, then squeezed himself by the flimsy door and out of sight. Eli smirked.

"I've changed my mind, Ray. I'm not going to kill you just yet. First I want to see the expression on that rugged, pretty mug of yours when you walk in on me doing to your fuck buddy, Connie, what that guy's doing here in the photo. Hey, don't look at me like that!" He purposely raised his voice in the hope Harry was outside the door, eavesdropping.

"I'm not a fucking homo! Fucking face is all the same, girl or boy. Learned that in the Youth Authority. But I do still prefer a woman's kisser to a man's any goddamn fucking day!"

On the outside, I kept my cool. But inside my head I had pictures of twisting Eli's noggin off like a rag doll's.

"Ray, don't look at me that way. I'm gettin' scared. You're gonna have me crappin' my drawers any second now."

He couldn't contain his laughter any longer. The sound was like the braying of a rabid donkey. It pushed something over the edge inside me, unleashing a red storm behind my eyes so that I could barely see him through the fury.

All of a sudden he saw something in my face, and it scared him. The hee-hawing see-sawed to a halt mid-bray, and he leapt to his feet. Keeping his eyes on me, the sadistic mirth disappeared, replaced by a reciprocal hatred that would have exploded into instant death for us both if either one of us had opened our mouth. I stepped aside. He absent-mindedly touched the inner thigh wound I'd given him earlier as he quickly edged his way into the vibrating corridor.

I don't remember too much that happened after that because I started feeling woozy. Part of it was probably seeing the creepy pictures, especially the one of Connie. That can do it to you, getting a Polaroid sprung on you by a mullet-headed psycho showing the love of your life blowing some guy. It can put you in a frame of mind – a blinding ache behind your eyes like your head's fit to burst and God knows what else. But somehow I don't think it can give you a stabbing cramp in your gut, a pain that feels like someone's begun a 24-hour-shift in your churning bowels with a jackhammer. That's what was coming on. I'm sure part of it was the blood I'd been covered with, some of which undoubtedly got inside me, not to mention the mescal hangover.

I stumbled the opposite way from where Eli and the queer Fed had gone, caroming shakily over itinerant workers and drunken musicians and squalling babies and their stone-faced Indian mothers. Somewhere in between cars, I started feeling faint, and the next thing I knew I was tumbling off the slow-moving train onto desert sands, getting bruised and scraped and throttled by mesquite, and that big, broiling, hellish lamp in the sky exploded into blackness.

PART TWO
Connie Eustace McQueen
August 1987

Chapter 12

Some people delight in being pricks. It's something I've ruminated on plenty of times since I've hit puberty. But it wasn't until a few days before my ordeal in New Orleans, when I was back working again at the strip club, that I really had the revelation come home to roost. Like a rattler hypnotizing chickens.

But I'm getting ahead of myself, as usual. I'll get to that in a bit. I probably should explain things first.

Ray had been gone a long time, but he'd called after his discharge and said he'd be home in no more than a month. That month was up three months ago. Making it four since I've heard from him.

I trust Ray. The fact that he's still gone does not bode well. The fact that he hasn't called to let me know if he's in trouble or if he's been delayed for some other reason especially does not bode well. I've been worried and am still worried sick. We've been going out since junior year in high school and here we are, both just shy of 30 and still hot for each other.

Ray is a bad boy, but he isn't a psychopath and he isn't a
sadist like most members of the male gender that pass through Mystic.
He's not near as bad as his mother, Lorna, who – well let's be fucking-
A honest, okay? – she's not been the best role model. She's a cheating
gambler and a ruthless hustler and a vicious thief and backstabbing
drug dealer, all with that charming back-country pancake-syrup style
of hers – and, oh yeah, she's the madam of one of the sleaziest, sickest
whorehouses this far south of Atlanta. Enough about her.

Ray isn't even as bad as washed-up Lucky Fordyce – Lucky
with his let-me-rip-off-as-a-many-poor-old-senior-citizens'-life's-
savings-scams-as-I-can. Telemarketing bullshit disguised as dummy-
company subsidiaries of his one legit mail-order business, selling his
greatest hits – all 20 of them. 20 golden gems of sixties and seventies
honky-tonk horseshit that I have to admit are still pretty listenable. But
just selling those records and cassettes – and I guess now those new
CDs – would not be enough to keep him and his fat slob of a manager
in the decadent lifestyle to which they have rather indulgently grown
accustomed. So they had to – at Lorna's suggestion, of course – start up
the under-the-table shit. I'm getting distracted, talking trash about
others.

Ray will occasionally rob a filling station or a liquor store or
even a bank if he's drunk enough. He'll sell drugs, including the hard
shit. But I know he hasn't killed – or wouldn't kill – anybody in cold
blood. At least, I don't think he would. He's got some lines he won't
cross.

I often try to wrap my head around why he ever enlisted in the
Navy in the first place. Not like him at all. I know the hot car stuff with
Jake and the coke-running for Lorna had been getting to him. Not like
he'd ever admit it. Down deep, I don't think he's cut out to be a
criminal. Which is a big reason why I love him. But coming from this
town and – worse – from Lorna, he didn't have a lot of choice.

What's happened to Ray? I wish I knew. I try not to think bad
thoughts, like maybe he's lying rotting in a shallow grave off some
highway crisscrossing the wastelands between here and Odessa. But
I've resigned myself. I'm powerless to do anything else.

I keep going back over my diary to see where and when this
whole thing really sent me off the rails. It was way before New
Orleans. I think I started sliding on that downhill slope even before Ray
called. He didn't know I was working for Lorna at the club. I had been
there for almost a year already when he got discharged in San Diego,

and it was eating away at me, knowing he was getting out, that he'd be calling to let me know when to expect him. And I'd been thinking on it, what the hell I was going to say, whether I would have the guts to tell him that I was stripping for his mother. Then he did call, and I just couldn't bring myself to break the news. I figured I'd wait; it would be better if I told him in person.

Over four months had gone by since I'd gotten his last call. I was drinking heavy all those months. I've always been able to keep up with the men, but I was going overboard, even for me.

One recent night an old redneck in bib overalls said something dirty, and I came down off the stage and upended his newly-filled pitcher of beer all over his sweaty, bald head. He'd taken me by the wrist and grabbed me down on his lap. Lee Simms and Mort Donegan, our bouncers, thought it was one big horselaugh. They stopped laughing when I swang the pitcher up between the fucker's legs and knocked him howling to the floor, puking his lunch out while he held onto his balls.

Janine had jumped off the stage and latched onto me before Mr. Greenjeans and his buddies could sober up enough to retaliate. She pulled me backstage, then out the rear door. We hid in her yellow GTO, locking it, Janine with her hand over my mouth, us both on the floor under a blanket in the back seat. We'd heard the drunken bastards roaring around, ping-ponging off the other cars in the lot, looking for us. Then things quieted down. They'd cooled off, gotten in their mud-splattered station wagon and fishtailed out of the gravel pasture onto the highway.

Ouch, my goddamn elbow hurts! And this fucking cast itches like crazy. In case you're wondering, I broke my arm a little while ago. Here I go again, getting ahead of myself. I'll get to how all that happened presently.

That night, the night we hid in Janine's GTO, she kissed me while we were under that blanket, and I felt myself getting wet. Her skin was beaded with sweat and so was mine and, what with our skimpy outfits, we were rubbing up against each other something fierce. For a minute I let myself go, and I gave into it, licking her big, thick lips and the creamy dark brown richness of her throat and shoulder. She smelled like lavender and sage and patchoulie, and that got me going even more. Then I started to get self-conscious and pushed her off of me.

"What's the matter, sugar?"

I sat up and peeked out. She reached over. I'd recently bleached my hair blonde, and she swept it aside to rub the back of my neck. I shrugged off her hand. "Looks like they're really gone."

"Hopefully they don't know where we live."

"It's almost closing time. Let's just book."

She frowned good-naturedly, nodded and drunkenly crawled like a spider over the back of the front seat, landing behind the steering wheel. She greedily grabbed a joint out of the glove compartment and torched up, inhaling deep, then offered it to me.

I waved it off as I sank into the back seat's ripped leather upholstery. "Nah-unh, not in the mood."

"Suit yourself." She reached down into her bikini panties, pulled out the car key, inserted it into the ignition and fired up the engine. A miniature dildo keyfob hung from it, lewdly dangling by the gearshift.

"That get you off, baby cakes, having that tucked in there snug as a bug in a rug while you're go-go dancing?"

She smiled a dirty smile into the rearview. "You better believe it. I'm always ready. Just you try me. Of all people, you should know."

I snorted, giggling at our filthy talk, making a joke out of the whole thing so I'd stop getting turned on. I'd made it a few times with Janine, but the last time I'd been with a guy was with Ray, right before he got inducted. And that's the way I aimed to keep it. We'd been faithful to each other the whole time we'd been together, a claim that 95% of the rest of the couples in Mystic could not truthfully make.

When we got to our little house on Maple, the lights were blazing and Wilson Pickett's *Mustang Sally* was blaring so loud you could hear it half a block away.

"What the fuck?"

"Shit!" Janine rammed the gear into park and frowned a petulant frown at the front yard.

I lost my temper. "You got to do something about Jeannie. Sis or not. I'm getting sick and tired of her breaking in all the time and having parties while we're at work. We kicked her out because of this crap. That's all we need now is for old man Kroger to evict us."

"Don't lecture me. I'm not any happier about it." She started to get out, then stopped as the door swung open. She sat down again and perched her chin on her elbow on the back of the seat, shooting me a honeyed smile. "You know we could stop worrying about all this if

you took Ray's mom up on her offer to rent us the place out on Rusty
Spring Wells."

"Fuck, Janey. I'm not getting beholden to Lorna for anything.
Why do you think that rent's so low? Moving in there would be the
slipperiest of slippery slopes. She'd have us talked into turning tricks
for her in no time."

She sighed.

"Christ-almighty," I went on, "How do you think Jeannie's
earning her keep? She's such a degenerate gambler drug addict."

"Don't rub it in."

"Ten-to-one she's shooting craps in there with Oliver and
Fitzroy right this goddamn minute."

Her eyes caught fire, and she jumped back to her feet. "All
right already! You preaching to the choir, girl!" She slammed the door
in my face as I started to fold the front seat forward to get out.

The screen door slammed, and then you could hear the twins
screaming at each other, their shouts louder than Wilson Pickett's.

By the time I got in the house, Janine was leaning against the
kitchen doorway, framed in silhouette, scowling angrily down at
Jeannie and her pals who were squatting in wide-legged stance,
shooting dice between the oven and the icebox.

I began loudly singing, "It's closing time…"

Janine echoed my sentiments. "C'mon, y'all, that's it."

Jeannie, Fitzroy, Oliver and another guy I didn't know – a
white guy with red hair and a nose that had been broken several times –
didn't pay us the slightest attention. Suddenly I recognized him. It was
Ernie Pyecroft. I hadn't seen him in at least ten years, and he was all
grown up into a man. He had a weird look in his eyes.

"Ernie." I unintentionally shouted. I knew he'd gotten back
from the army a couple of years ago, but he never came into town. Just
stayed at home taking care of his ten-year-old sister, April. His pa was
god knows where, and his mama Maggie was in the penitentiary for at
least another eighteen months, finishing up a sentence for mail fraud.

He raised his eyes to meet mine.

"What're you doing here? Leaving your sister home alone?"

"She's okay." He smiled uncertainly at my question, then
frowned and returned his attention to the game, muttering under his
breath, "She can take better care of herself than me."

Janine chimed in. "All of you going home anyway. Game's
over."

Jeannie shot a hateful glance at the both of us. "Goddamn it, these boys got my money. I need to win it back 'fore a one of them leaves this goddamn fuckin' house."

Oliver chimed in. "You mean Ernie's got yer money. Mother-fucker got mine and Fitz's, too."

Ernie smirked and came out with a lopsided grin that exposed his missing front teeth. "Janey's right, boys, time we called it a night, don' you think?" He drawled it out slow and syrupy as he snatched all the bills from the grimy floor with his even grimier fist.

Fitzroy threw out one massive palm and closed it over Ernie's balled-up hand.

"Gimmie a look-see at the dice, man. Somethin' ain' right."

Ernie's arm yanked back with a jerk that slammed his elbow into the fridge door, jarring the appliance so the cereal boxes on top fell off, disappearing behind it.

Oliver got distracted when he saw that all Janine and I had on were our skimpy club outfits under our jackets. But Fitzroy and Jeannie homed in on Ernie, murder in their eyes. I didn't like the feeling I was getting. Ernie sauntered sideways, keeping his face towards them, then he edged behind my back. He suddenly grabbed my arms and threw me at Fitzroy and, before I knew it, I was hearing the front screen door slam. Fitzroy bounced me into Jeannie, then he, too, was off like a shot.

"Goddamn motherfucker." Jeannie revved herself up, taking off, but Janine was too fast, clamping her hands around both her sister's arms from behind.

"You stayin' right here, girl."

Jeannie tried to whip around, snarling and spitting like a cat.

"Go on, Ollie." I said to our leering admirer, as serious as I could. "Get on home."

He looked at Janine, and she nodded, ignoring her struggling twin. Oliver squeezed past us, frightened, then was gone.

"You goddamn bitch, lemme go."

Janine ignored her and gave me a questioning look. "You thinkin' what I'm thinkin'?"

I grimaced. "Something bad's gonna happen."

"If Fitz catches Ernie."

I let out a deep breath. "I'm gonna mosey up the street a ways and see what's happening."

"You look out for yourself. Both those boys have knives."

Jeannie lashed out with her face, trying to bite me, but only her wild mane of stiff, unwashed hair connected. "Goddamn you cunts!"

There was only one streetlight burning, a yellow orb filtering through
the green haze of a massive oak on the corner where Maple
bisected Sundown. I heard their angry shouting voices – Fitz and
Ernie's – further down, maybe two blocks, but I couldn't see them.
The neighborhood, too, was alive with cries of "I'm trying to sleep,
goddamn it!" "Shut the fucking hell up, you goddamn sons-of-fucking
bitches!" and "Jesus Lord, mercy, it's after one o'clock, you godless
men!"

I was still a little drunk. The night was cooling and sobering
me, though the humid air felt like a wet sheet wrapped around my face.
The clip clop of my heels sounded a hollow echo against the pock-
marked pavement. There's no sidewalks in our neighborhood, so I was
walking down the middle of the road.

Smells were wafting up all around me. I am always sensitive to
smell, but when I'm drunk, the odors come on stronger. I could smell
the garbage, acrid, sour, sulphurous and gag-inducing, as I passed
McClain's cluttered-with-debris front yard, then the cloying sweetness
of the huge magnolia tree in Mrs. Grady's.

I stepped into a pothole and, by some unforeseen grace, kept
from twisting my ankle. I raised my foot and adjusted my high-heel
fuck-me pumps so they faced down again. A wave of nausea swept over
me, aided and abetted by the malodorous neighborhood. I stayed
doubled-over, my hands on my knees, and concentrated on deep
breaths.

Why the fuck was I following these two?

The just-about-to-hurl feeling left almost as quickly as it had
come. And for whatever stupid, altruistic reason, I kept right on after
them. They were headed in the direction of Ernie's house, which was
about a half mile outside town, beyond the first stretch of woods, a
decaying homestead masquerading as a farm. It was in a clearing along
the narrow two-lane blacktop, slightly uphill to the northeast.

I quickened my pace.

Still, I wondered what the hell I was going to be able to do
when – and if – I caught up to them. I had no weapons except my sharp
tongue.

Another two blocks, and the recognizable structure of Mystic,
our little misbegotten town, started to gradually fall away. I became
acutely aware I was clad only in a knee-length leather jacket, bikini and
heels, and that was it. I could handle one guy, unless there was a gun
involved. But I was worried about more than one. And knowing the

neighborhood, I could guarantee that Ernie and Fitz weren't the only lunatics at large.

Then I heard their voices clear as a bell.

"Gimmie that fifty dollar, you no account, cracker peckerhead! Those dice of yers are crooked!"

"Fitz, I'm disappointed you choosin' to stoop to low racial stereotypes over a minor disagreement on financial matters."

They were facing off under the cover of a huge oak that jutted its darkening branches all the way across the road. Ernie was backed up against the trunk, with Fitz slowly closing in.

"Fitz." I muttered.

They both jumped as if tapped by a live wire. Fitz threw a quick glance over his shoulder, but his eyes zeroed back in on Ernie as he heard him shuffling to one side.

"Connie, get the hell out of here. This ain't none of yer goddamn business."

"The hell it ain't. It started up in my kitchen, and it should have ended there."

"Fuck you, girl."

"Don't talk to me that way, Fitz. I thought we were friends."

"We was friends till now. A friend wouldn't ask me to back down when I been ripped off. So, I guess you ain't a friend after all."

"Give me that knife."

He didn't answer. The two of them just stood there, frozen, staring each other down.

"You should listen to her. She tryin' to talk sense." Ernie's voice was nervous, no longer slurred with drink.

"Only sense to be talkin' is for that fifty dollar to come back out your shoe and into my pocket."

"The hell!"

Fitz laughed. "The hell you say? That's right, peckerwood. That's where yer headed in about two-and-a-half minutes if I don't see the long green."

"You a mean son-of-a-bitch, Fitz. I won that money fair and square. My dice ain't crooked." It looked like Ernie was reaching for something in his shirt pocket. He threw a couple of tiny somethings – the dice, I guess – on the leaf-littered ground at Fitz's feet. "Take a look, goddamn it!"

With the split second that Fitz cast down his eyes, Ernie sprang off the trunk of the oak and went shooting up the road towards his place. Before Fitz could tear after him, I grabbed onto his arm, probably not the smartest thing I could have done under the circumstances. He whirled, slashing at me with the blade and just narrowly missing my bare stomach. When I lunged backwards to keep from being ventilated, I tripped on a branch and fell on my ass. Looking up, I could barely make out Fitz disappearing into the mist at the crest of the road.

I got to my feet, slipped off my heels so I could carry them, dusted myself off and began running.

Ernie's place was closer than I thought. I was out of breath, but I knew I hadn't run that far, probably no more than a quarter of a mile. I knew I was near because suddenly Ernie's ten-year-old sister, little redheaded April, was sailing into me out of the darkness, weeping. I caught her in my arms and, at first, she fought me, thinking I was someone who meant to do her harm. Then I called her name close to her ear, holding and caressing her hair, telling her she was safe.

"Ernie and some black guy are fightin' in the corral!"

I took her by the hand, and we ran back up the slight hill, only to nearly miss being trampled by two horses who were bolting out of the fog, bearing down on us at a thunderous gallop. I clutched at April, shoving her behind me as the two bellowing, snorting beasts veered off on either side.

We both stood stock-still for almost a full minute, hearing only our own excited breaths, then the lowing of a cow not too far distant and then the two men's angry voices echoing across to us. I stepped forward three or four paces, and the Pyecroft farm came into sight.

The corral gate was open. A battered '72 model Dodge truck, jacked up, missing both rear tires, was parked on the nearest side of the now empty pen. The Pyecroft milk cow peeked around at me from the front of the vehicle, mooing to show its fear and annoyance. I suddenly felt April's tiny hand slip into mine, and I looked down at her, hidden slightly behind me on my left. She had her other hand raised to cover her mouth in consternation.

Through the corral, on the other side – its fourth wall – was the ramshackle two-story house itself. What I supposed to be the kitchen screen door was gaping open. There was a bloodcurdling cry from inside, then silence.

"You stay here, honey," I crouched slightly to look her in the eye, "I'm heading in there to see what's going on."

"I don't want to stay here by myself."

"You'll be safer here, sweetheart. Okay? I won't be but a minute."

"'Spose he got Ernie, then he gets you?"

I tried to smile at the sobering thought, "He ain't gonna get me, honey. I'm good at taking care of myself."

I left her standing there before she could put up any more protests and crept as quietly as I could towards the back door.

Right before I climbed onto the two rickety, split boards that served as steps, I stared up at the full moon. It burned with a cold white fire in a purple velvet sky full of twinkling silver specks.

I squinted, rubbed the bridge of my nose and wished that I had had another drink. Chances are, I thought, Ernie has plenty of shine liquor close by. But I don't know where it is, so it won't do me a damn bit of good.

The very warm breeze became a wind that swayed the flexing branches of the woods across the dirt road. The sweet aroma of black walnut, red maple and green ash filled the thick air. Boughs of dry leaves whispered. I noticed a gradual upswelling of ragged breathing coming from within the kitchen or just beyond it, and the faint flickering of fluorescent light raised the hairs on the back of my neck.

Before I ventured inside, I spotted a broken, overturned wooden chair, a cast-iron frying pan and a shattered plate on the garbage-strewn floor. It took me a few seconds to take it all in. There was no one in the trashed room, but sure enough, they'd passed through on their way to some greater glory.

A voice groaned and moaned – Fitz's voice.

"Goddamn you, Ernie, you egg-sucking, gas-huffin' bitch!" The sound was filled with pain – gasping, mewling, twisted, insane. "Why'd you do such thing?"

Then I noticed a trail of something, a drip-drop of viscous black muck that I abruptly realized was a thread of fresh blood, leading along the greasy linoleum and brick surface, splattering in a generous pool before the ancient hearth, then continuing spiderweb-like, on, on and on beside the rotting-food-cluttered kitchen table, pointing the way to me so I could track my quarry. I sidestepped to keep out of the blood, but as I rounded the corner into the dark hall and saw a shimmering circle of yellow light spill from a room a few feet to my left, I pranced into a sticky glob of it.

"Who that out there, goddamn it! I got me a knife!"

I peered into what was the bathroom but what could more accurately be described as a chamber of horrors. Fitz was still on his feet, in a partial crouch, doubled-over with literally stabbing cramps in his right side. A long, rusty barbeque fork protruded from his ripped shirt. Ernie was on his knees, his front half slumped into the gory bathtub, and I knew right away he was dead. Ernie's giant fork in Fitz's side had not deterred his pursuer, only spurred him on to all-out mayhem. Ernie's throat had been cut from behind, from ear to ear and, even though he was beyond help and would soon be growing cold, I could spot his red life still draining out of him onto the now crimson enamel. The shock of so much gore hit me like a fist in the stomach and, without any warning nausea, I puked all over the hall floor. I wiped my mouth with my hand, never letting my eyes stray from Fitz, whose attention had shifted to me.

"Girl, you a damn fool followin' us up here. You gonna make me kill you, too?"

Fitz tried to straighten but couldn't. He stared an icy stare at me, his eyes still full to the brim with murder. Tears of anger and despair mingled with sweat on his cheeks. He stumbled towards me, wrenching the grill fork from his side and brandishing his knife, now dulled with blood. I backed up as he shambled out of the bathroom. At any second, I knew he could lunge and thrust the blade into my chest. The seconds ticked by like hours as I did a clumsy, backward dance through the foul-smelling kitchen. Suddenly I had an instinct of when the time was right and bolted, jumping outside into the night and slamming the screen door behind me. Meanwhile, poor little April had come closer, trembling with fear, and I caught her in my arms mid-corral, plunging through the open gate and making a beeline for the tree cover of the forest about ten yards away.

"Girl, you can't run from me!" Fitz tried to roar out his rage as he hobbled to the edge of the corral, but his voice came out as more of a croak.

We had just gone behind a towering chestnut tree when a car's high beams swept across the woods and the road, coming to rest on shellshocked Fitz propping himself up on one rear fender of Ernie's out-of-commission truck. Gravel crunched and raked with flying pebbles as Sheriff Brody Van Heusen stomped on his brakes and popped out of his cruiser. He immediately leveled a shotgun at Fitz.

"Throw down your weapon, boy."

Fitz stared dumbly at him. Then he called out in fear, "Connie, where you girl? You gonna stand by and watch him murder me?"

I gulped.

"Connie, goddamn it!"

Van Heusen looked uncertainly around the yard, the corral and then over towards the trees before finally returning his stare to his sitting duck target.

"Somebody else out here with you, boy?"

Fitz didn't answer.

"You got a female accomplice hidin' some place nearby?" He craned his head and shouted. "Anybody else out there? Better speak now or forever hold your peace." He shrugged. "Better tell me where they is, Fitzroy. I figure since I don't see Ernie anywhere, an' you covered head to toe in blood with a gory knife in yer hand, you guilty of some mighty serious lawbreakin'."

"Fuck you, you pie-shovelin' cracker."

There was a deafening explosion as Van Heusen let him have it with both barrels, and Fitz splattered all over the Dodge's tailgate. I clamped my hand over April's eyes and mouth as I backed us further into the trees. Thankfully Van Heusen was by himself. He grabbed hold of the spotlight mounted on the side of his windshield, switched it on and let it play over the corral, the house, the far side of the yard, the crippled Dodge truck. By the time he swung it round in our direction in the trees, we were another 15 yards or so further into the brambles and briars. Our legs were getting scratched, and little April was whimpering softly. Several owls hooted, and the last thing I saw through the shifting branches was Van Heusen stepping up into the house through the back kitchen door.

Chapter 13

I shifted a bit because a knot in the old oak tree I was propped against was digging into my left shoulder blade. I tried to be as subtle as I could with my movement because I didn't want to wake April, who was sound asleep, curled in my lap with my arms around her.

Unwelcome images of Ernie's and Fitz's bloody demise banged their way into my head, and I chased them right out again, anxious about another kind of death.

With the warm weather, it being night or not, I was worried about snakes. It was so warm out, they might not have all been in their holes. Our countryside has plenty of poisonous ones, copperheads and cottonmouths and especially rattlers, for which our town is famed.

For years and years, Mystic used to hold a rattlesnake round-up every summer: hunters, sportsmen and hillbillies, townfolk and snake handlers, conservationists and hippies, all descending in a drunken debauch for an ungodly weekend of trapping the poor venomous things in their lairs. Their unforgiving capture and massacre of the reptiles had kept the snake population well under control. But then the round-ups ended. I'll spare you the details. The town had given up the whole idea in the early 1970s when one of Mystic's own favorite sons had gone off his rocker and committed mass homicidal mayhem on a number of folks. The killer's whole family had blown apart that summer, and it was like someone had let the air out of a balloon. That one weekend had been so full of carnage – the sheriff had been murdered the day before by a crazy girl – it had left a bad taste in everyone's mouth. Which, for Mystic, is saying a lot. It takes an awful lot to leave a bad taste in Mystic's collective mouth.

I'm – what do you call it? – digressing.

I hadn't seen any snakes at all, though I'd heard all kinds of nightlife skulking and slithering and creeping through the brush. The frogs were croaking and singing, nightbirds were hooting and warbling, and cicadas and crickets were screeching and chirping.

I remember looking down at that poor little forlorn thing curled up in my arms. Seeing her there, so alone and vulnerable, reminded me of my parents and how they had died.

I'd just turned seventeen.

Daddy had been letting me drive their second car, an old Buick. It was a moonless night, they were ahead in the Oldsmobile, and I was following them. We were moving to a new house.

Daddy was a doctor and his practice had finally taken off. He was a good, responsible man and always kind to me. Oh, sometimes he'd get a little crazy, flying off the handle when he was drunk, which wasn't very often. But I thought at the time all grown-ups were like that. And even though I'd already started going out with Ray – and had met his parents – I didn't know yet that most of them were much, much worse. My mama? Smart, but not too smart. Uneducated, overtly religious – we were Catholic, too, which set us apart; not too many Catholics in Mystic – and she was what I'd guess most educated people would call really, really neurotic. Roe v Wade had just happened, and she was one of the first of the obsessive anti-abortion activists. She used to drive me nuts the way she'd talk about it all the time.

That night, they were ahead three or four car lengths when it began to rain. There was heavy thunder and lightning. Ten minutes further on we suddenly came up on a railroad crossing. The lights weren't flashing, but Daddy slowed down and stopped just as he always did. He was always careful when he was driving. Then he slowly started across. Before the car cleared halfway, there was the locomotive's bright headlight bearing down on them, its horn blaring, its engine roaring out of the blackness, smashing the Olds and crumpling it like an accordion as it rammed the car another quarter mile down the tracks. I remember the explosion of the gas tank, the sparks from the train wheels as it threw on its emergency brakes. I was told much later at the inquest that a lightning strike had shorted out the crossing's warning lights. It was all a matter of bad timing.

At least I was almost out of high school when I became an orphan. Not like the poor little thing in my lap. I had been thrown in an icy pond kind of hell. I somehow resolved not to let the water freeze back over me, keeping me from surfacing and surviving. But I was underwater for a long time. First, in a cocoon of numbness, then a blossoming of excruciating torment – the gut-sucking torment of inexplicable, irretrievable loss.

My mother's sister, a widow, Aunt Vivian from Hattiesburg, came to live with me at the new house. The place was left to me, but I was still in school. Daddy had already made a huge down payment, and Aunt Viv got a job as a ticketseller and concession girl at the local drive-in movie. I worked at Woolworth's for a few hours on weekdays after my classes. We barely managed to make the mortgage each month and keep pork and beans on the table. We managed to fend off the foreclosure vultures for almost three years.

About that time, Aunt Viv got diagnosed with diabetes and went blind. She had to stop working. She'd been a lot like Mama before that, religious and uptight. She didn't dig Ray too much, but at least she let me keep seeing him. When she lost her sight, she was very angry at first, and treated me like shit. Then one night I let her have it. She broke down, and the next morning she apologized.

Gradually, she loosened up. Her new loneliness and vulnerability softened her. If I'd been forced to take odds before her diabetes, if somebody had asked me how she would react to something like that, I would have said poisonous bile and bitterness. But I was wrong; her hard shell cracked, and she became more warm and human. Maybe even capable of love.

Eventually, though, the no-money problem got to be too much for the both of us. We got evicted. By then I was nearly 21 and went to live at Ray's – really his mama Lorna's – house. Aunt Viv went back to Hattiesburg to live with cousins.

Ray's daddy Rolo was gone by then, struck down by a sudden heart attack. Rolo had been a hot-tempered, frustrated man who'd wanted to be a lawyer but had gotten roped into running the family appliance business when his father had died. Inheriting the business, selling refrigerators and gas stoves, made him rich, at least for most of the remainder of his life. Unfortunately, he'd married Lorna, an ex-Nashville hooker he was head-over-heels on. Ray was born five months later. When Rolo was drunk, he'd sometimes wonder aloud if he was really Ray's dad. That didn't do much for Ray's outlook on life. Things started to unravel financially about a year before he died. I'd always thought Lorna's extravagant lifestyle hadn't exactly contributed anything positive towards Rolo's good health. Too bad that his financial affairs were in such a mess when he kicked the bucket. The business went bankrupt, and Lorna and Ray would have been left pretty much penniless if Ray hadn't been working at Jake Platt's garage. Luckily the mortgage on their two-story mansion was already paid.

Lorna soon returned to the larcenous habits of her youth to bring in extra cash – kiting checks, selling drugs, even turning tricks with high rollers. And she was only too glad for me to move in when I lost my house. I was at Woolworth's full time by then and could contribute to putting bread on the table. Even though I'd been an A student, college was out for me.

I didn't last too long at Woolworth's. My wild, partying life-style with Ray was starting to kick in. And, as much as I didn't trust Lorna, there was a part of me that admired her. My bad-girl side, I guess. She was not a great influence.

I'd always had a strong suspicion that mama Lorna was one of the reasons daddy Rolo's business went belly up, that she'd been embezzling funds into her own account. After all, she'd been Rolo's bookkeeper, and I'd heard plenty of tales in Rolo's final months about how figures weren't adding up like they should. When Lorna bought a sleazy honky tonk roadhouse out on Route 5 two years after Rolo went in the ground, my suspicions were pretty much confirmed. Her partner on the deal was her old Nashville pal, country star Lucky Fordyce.

I stopped thinking about all that.

Seeing Ernie and Fitz suddenly killed had sobered me, made me realize things were getting way out of hand in my circle of friends. The problem was I didn't really fit in with any of the cliques in Mystic. You had the hard-scrabble, righteously religious contingent – poor, middle class or well-to-do didn't matter – who judged everyone by appearances and were largely a bunch of hypocrites; and you had the hard-drinking, corrupt, racist sociopaths – many middle class and rich, but just as many poor white and black trash – who were liars, cheats and sometimes killers. Then there was the small, comparatively young crowd of "hip" drinking and drugging miscreants who loved to party – long live any kind of outlaw music from rock 'n' roll to R&B to country blues. These were folks who were certainly not on the right side of the law but didn't indulge their criminality on anywhere near the scale of the more illustrious crooked citizens. I guess I came closest to fitting in that last category. To be fair, there was also a small handful – and I mean small – of people who were "decent" and hard-working, intent on minding their own business and staying out of the way of the rest of us.

My crowd was fast-imploding. There was the smothering sense of a community slowly dying on the vine all over Mystic; it had been that way for at least ten years. Our bunch were self-indulgent creatures dedicated to living exclusively in the here-and-now, seeking earthly pleasures of the senses because we – maybe rightly – believed, and still do believe, that there's no tomorrow. But easy income for the indolent was steadily decreasing by the month. An unacknowledged, low-key desperation was settling into all our bones, and no better proof existed than what had happened to Ernie and Fitz that very night. Something had to give. I wanted to find a way out, but I wasn't sure how. I didn't want to give up on Ray. But I didn't want to die, either. Which I figured could happen very easily the way things were going.

I stared up at the moon, huge, full, fearfully bright and glowing in the indigo sky, and I closed my eyes. After a couple of minutes, I stretched out my hand, and I imagined I could touch it. My fingers felt a soft, clammy, wet surface, and I reopened my lids. The moon's surface was mere inches from my face, and my fingertips were mired in the yellow, melted cheese-like surface. Then I realized there were huge eyes there in the moon, weeping rivers of tears and staring down at me accusingly.

I fitfully started and realized I'd fallen asleep. When I awoke, I saw that April was standing on my lap, clutching my right hand to her face, crying softly. I hugged her to me.

"What's the matter, sweetie? Don't be afraid now. You're safe with me."

"Something bad happened, I know."

"Yes, darling, but you're okay."

"But what happened to Ernie?"

"Ernie went on a long trip. He had to go. He won't be back anytime soon."

"No!"

I nodded, fighting back tears myself, unable to tell her anything closer to the truth.

"I don't like it out here. It's scary."

All at once, I realized I must have been asleep longer than I

thought. The moon was down, and I could see through the trees that
there was a faint glimmer of dawn in the distance.

"You know what, honey? I don't like it out here, either."

I stood, picking her up and setting her on the ground by the old,
eaten-away hollow cypress that had fallen long ago next to the giant
oak. I brushed myself off, then took her hand in mine. I led her through
the woods back the way we came, then paused when I could glimpse
the Pyecroft house through the overhanging branches. Fitz's body was
gone, although there was a dark red, almost black splash-mark left on
the rear of the truck where he'd been splattered by Brody Van Heusen's
scattergun. Yellow crime tape ranged from far to the left in front of the
old Dodge, curling around it, then encircling the whole corral,
disappearing on the other side to the right, symbolically prohibiting
entry into the crime scene. No other vehicles or signs of life were
visible.

I stood there for a few minutes, leery of emerging too soon.
The night before, for just a few moments, Van Heusen had thought
someone else besides Ernie really had been there with Fitz. Then again,
I doubt he would have killed Fitz so coldbloodedly if he hadn't
believed himself unobserved. Unless he had just lost his temper, which
would not have been out of character.

Nothing happened, so April and I left the trees and started
walking down the middle of the road. I didn't want to be seen
coming into town on that thoroughfare, so as soon as we got closer
to the DeRosie brothers' vast pasture, we cut across it. I was on okay
terms with the brothers, had gone to school with them, and even if they
didn't approve of my lifestyle, I knew they weren't snitches. We could
cut through their farm and hit the other road that would bring us down
further south on Maple.

The brothers weren't anywhere in sight and neither were most
of the cows. The farm was a milking operation and had a couple of long
narrow barns for the purpose. The whole area smelled like cowshit and,
beyond the fence to our left, closer to the road, teenage kids – both boys
and girls – were playing football. I couldn't believe they were up so
goddamn early. You never would have caught me or Ray ever getting
up at that hour to do something idiotic like play sports. I recognized the
lion's share of the boys and knew for a fact they were high schoolers
who hadn't been able to cut it on the regular team. One or two of them
glanced over but, for the most part, they ignored us.

We walked between the main house and the barns, heading
down the DeRosie's long dirt drive that came out on Sage Avenue,

which would weave around for about a quarter mile and spill us out on
Maple about a block from my house. We didn't run into a soul. The sun
was already leaving a nasty impression, gearing up into nuclear
meltdown mode. I hadn't been up so early in I don't know how long.
Quite often I went to sleep at dawn and woke up in the late afternoon.

"Where we goin'?"

"My house. We'll fix you some breakfast cereal. That sound
good, honey?"

She nodded, getting distracted by a cloud of dust further down
Sage.

"You got any other kin, sweetheart? Besides Ernie and your
mama?"

"Got an aunt and uncle and some cousins in Macon."

"You ever stay over with them?"

"Not in a while."

"Think they'd let you stay for a time?"

She shrugged. "Dunno. Maybe."

Then a sheriff's car pulled up, and Deputy Sonny Jessup lazily
got out and sauntered over to us, his thumbs hooked in his gunbelt.
Thank God it wasn't Van Heusen.

I leaned down a bit and whispered to April, "Don't tell him
anything about me being up at your place last night, okay, sugar?"

Sonny butted in. "What's the haps, Connie? You up a little
early."

"Couldn't sleep and went for a walk."

"Hhm. That so? Who's your friend?" He knelt down on one
knee in front of the shy little girl.

"This wouldn't be young April Pyecroft, would it?"

He looked at me, but I just squinted at him, shielding my eyes
from the glare of the rising sun. He winked at April. "Are you Ernie's
sis?"

She nodded.

"I just ran into her a minute ago," I explained, "Coming out the
DeRosie's drive."

Sonny ignored me. "You been outside all night, honey? You
got a lot of brambles and weeds in your socks and sweater there." He
glanced at me. Luckily my leather jacket didn't collect vegetation like
April's cotton fabric did. "You ain't got much on under that jacket,
Connie."

"Didn't expect to run into anybody this early."

"That there, underneath, 's your club outfit, ain't it?"

I didn't answer.

"Ain't it?"

"Sometimes."

He stood up and looked me in the eye.

"I heard there was a spot of trouble out there last night. One of the dancers did a little damage between some shitheel's legs. Not that he probably didn't ask for it. Of course, you wouldn't know anything about that, would you?"

I just kept looking at him.

He finally broke eye contact and stared at April, patting her on the head. "Well, we need to take this little one to the station in town. Ask her some questions after she's had her breakfast." He paused, then squinted at me. "Some considerably worse things happened out at the Pyecroft place last night. I won't go into the details in front of her."

April tugged on his pant leg. "Where did Ernie go?"

I bit my lip.

Sonny gave me a thoughtful look but answered her. "Ernie had himself a bad night, honey." He knelt beside her again. "You weren't there?"

"I ran out the door when Ernie and a black man started into fighting. I ain't seen Ernie since." She started to cry and turned to me, hugging my legs. I put one hand on her head, smoothing her messed up tangle of auburn hair.

He picked her up away from me, slinging her so she was sitting on his massive right forearm, and she automatically laid her head on his shoulder. He angled towards the cruiser with her and frowned as he gave me a backward glance.

"Don't 'spose you know anything about Ernie, either."

"When Janine and I got back from the club last night, we found him at the house throwing dice with Fitzroy. We told them time and again not to be gambling at our place, throwing dice, so we kicked them out. They were having an argument when they left."

"Oh, really?" He put April in the passenger side of the cruiser's front seat, then gently shut the door as he walked back to me. "About what time was this?"

I shrugged. "Maybe 1 or 1:30. I was kind of half in the bag."

"As usual." He gazed out towards where the kids were playing ball. "You want me to give you a ride back to your house, since it's on the way?" He tilted and turned his face, giving me a strange, flirty smile.

"Don't suppose so, Sonny. You know I'm kind of allergic to the back seats of cop cars."

He nodded. "Thought so."

I laughed, nervous. "Besides, I need the exercise."

"Don't get enough of that onstage at the club, hunh?"

"A girl needs to sweat out the toxins, soaking up all that cheap liquor."

He nodded. After he'd opened his door, he seemed to have an afterthought, looked in at April, then out at me and shut the door so she couldn't hear. Once again, he came a few paces closer.

"Some really bad things happened to Ernie and Fitz out at the Pyecroft house. Really, really bad things. Bloody things. Guess their argument about the dice got out of hand."

He shot a cold stare at me for several seconds, then stepped to the car and, in one suave, smooth motion, swung open the door, sank into the driver's seat and switched the car on. He backed up, turned it around and headed into town.

I drew my arm across my forehead.

I was dripping with sweat.

Chapter 14

When I got back to the house, there was the oppressive air of closed-up, shut-in, super-heated darkness, the ever-increasing violence of a merciless sun trying to enter through the rotting drapes. During these kinds of suffocating summer months, Ray used to call it our own personal death star, homing in for the kill.

As my eyes adjusted to the faint light, I noticed a figure on the couch. At first, I wasn't sure if it was Janine.

"Hello, stranger."

I sighed with relief.

"Whatsamsatter? Think I was Jeannie?"

I nodded.

"She headed out about an hour after you left. I was too damn tired to hold onto her any longer and figured it wouldn't do any harm by then."

Janine lit a joint and sucked in a lungful of sharp smoke. Her voice raspily deepened as she held it, then spoke. "Girl, I was worried you'd gone the way of all flesh."

"You already heard?"

She nodded, taking another hit. "Lorna called."

"Figures. She knows everything."

"Even before it happens." She sarcastically whispered the

words as she offered me the joint, and I unthinkingly took it. "She wanted you to come out to see her as soon as you got in."

My heart felt like someone had suddenly squeezed it tightly in their fist. I returned the joint without partaking. "That's all I fuckin' need. I'm sure as hell not gonna go out there stoned."

She laughed. "Why the hell not? I thought you liked horror movies. Especially when you're high."

I sank down beside her on the sagging couch.

She got serious. "Did you see what happened?"

I nodded. "It was pretty fuckin' bad. Never saw anyone killed before, not like that. Two people at one time."

"What about your parents?"

"With them it was like…one minute they're there, the next, they're gone. It was dark and pouring rain. Their car suddenly just disappeared, slammed down the tracks by the locomotive. I was lucky. They didn't make me ID their bodies…what was left of them."

"Yeah?"

"So, I take it you want a blow-by-blow on Ernie and Fitz?"

She frowned at my grouchy sarcasm, and I immediately regretted it.

"I'm sorry. I slept in the woods, hiding out with little April, Ernie's sister. Then we ran into Deputy Sonny on the way back, out near the DeRosie Brothers' place. He took her with him."

"Whew. And he let you go? You lucky, sweetie. Lucky it wasn't that son-of-a-bitch, Van Heusen."

"The same thought had crossed my mind." I closed my eyes. "It was a bloodbath out at Ernie's. Stupid SOB stabbed Fitz in the side with a barbecue fork, then somehow Fitz overpowered him and cut his throat."

"Goddamn."

"I made April stay outside and went in the back door right after it happened. Fitz came at me, but I managed to take off. I snatched April, and we hightailed it into the trees. Right as we hit cover, Van Heusen pulls up and jumps out of his cruiser with a scattergun."

"Motherfucker."

"He tells Fitz to drop his knife, and he doesn't. But Fitz *does* fucking start yelling my name –"

"Damn."

"– going, 'Hey, Connie, you aiming to let him murder me?' Van Heusen is all confused because he doesn't think anyone else is out there with Fitz. Then Fitz basically tells him to fuck off, and Van Heusen lets loose with both barrels."

I sat forward and rested my elbows on my knees, exhaling a deep, exhausted breath, then, as afterthought, shrugged out of my jacket.

"I think Van Heusen thought maybe there was someone else around, but since he was solo, he decided to go investigate in the house instead, see what mayhem Fitz had got into. I dragged April deep into the woods, and we fell asleep. Woke up right as the sun was about to come up."

"Hell. Maybe you should lay low at Lorna's for a while."

"Not a chance."

"Maybe she'll stake you to get out of town."

"You living in a fairy tale?"

"You never know. Van Heusen may come looking for you. Especially when he hears from Sonny you were with April right after sun-up."

I changed the subject, "I hadn't seen Ernie in years, till last night."

"Can't believe Ernie and Fitz finally exploded like that. You may not have seen Ernie around because he stopped coming to the Milk Train right before you got hired. He had a thing for Brenda Lee Lake —"

"Jesus, no shit? Poor son-of-a-bitch."

"Yeah, raked him over the coals and tore him down. You never go to the roadhouse, to Sleepy Eyes, so you wouldn't know, but after Ernie stopped hitting the Milk Train, coming to gawk at the strippers in place of Brenda, he started showin' there instead. Hangin' in the back room where Lorna's got the slots and the poker and craps tables. He and Fitz were gambling against each other regular. Got into it plenty, but never came to blows. Not that I heard."

Our cat, Mur, that I'd raised since she could fit snug in the palm of my hand, jumped in my lap and started licking and chewing playfully my fingers. Somehow she opened a place in my heart right then, and a sudden, horrible pang of longing welled up in me for Ray's embrace. For a few seconds, I thought I was going to get weepy.

"That damn little fool loves you."

I stroked Mur's fur. It was marked with long, elegant streaks of grey and black that looked like liquid marble. I remembered nursing her when she was only a few weeks old, cleaning out her pus-filled, glued-together eyelids twice a day with the Q-tips and antibiotic drops until she got over the infection. "She may be two years old, but she's still a kitten in her head."

"It's the water, sugar. You know how those environmentalists go on about the toxic waste from the McCarr-Lee site leeching into the ground table? McCarr-Lee always assuring the public that Mystic's water supply is safe, that all these cases of cancer in Mystic are just coincidental? The water, honey, it fucks up everything. Eats away inside," she jabbed a thumb into her chest, "Makes everything backward. And mentally deficient."

"Including us?"

"We're still living here, ain't we? Can't have too many brains left to be doing that."

I stood up shakily, "I'm going to take a shower, then head over to Lorna's. Might as well get it over with."

"I would if I were you."

"Can you drop me?"

She nodded as she lit the roach and finished it.

The Diamond residence, what was now Lorna's place, looked a lot like the house in *Texas Chainsaw Massacre*. You know, the one where Leatherface and his family lived? I'd always thought that. And the resemblance became more and more striking as the years ticked by because Lorna, despite her ill-gotten gains, didn't really keep the place up, at least on the outside. It didn't do much to lighten my spirits, spying the house in the distance at the end of the drive, looming larger through the GTO windshield.

Janine tried to sound an optimistic note. "Ray's got to be back soon."

"At this point, whether he shows or not, I don't know how much difference it'll make. The way everything is going downhill."

"Gotta stop thinking like that, honey. Elsewise just blow your brains out now and be done with it."

I smiled. I supposed she was right. I got out and joked, "I guess it's that toxic groundwater put me in this frame of mind."

She laughed. "Call me later if you want me to pick you up."

I nodded, shut the door and waved as she slammed the car in reverse and backed it down the gravel path at a fast, crunching clip.

The front door was wide open, and the screen door in front of it was unlocked. I didn't need to knock, virtually being Lorna's daughter-in-law, but I did anyway, rapping lightly. There was a low murmur of voices coming from the living room. Minutes ticked by, and no one appeared, so I pulled open the screen and stepped in.

Off to the left, Lucky Fordyce and Lorna had converted the
living and dining rooms into the packaging and marketing department
for Lucky's albums, their combo TV ads and telemarketing operation.
Lucky was perched, one cowboy-boot leg dangling, on the edge of
a long table where two women sat in mini-dresses with beehive
bouffant hairdos. The girls were inserting CDs of Lucky's Greatest
Hits into plastic bubble-cushioned mailers, raptly listening to Lucky's
litany of being-on-the-road war stories. Beyond them, at the far end,
where there should have been a homey dining room with table and
chairs, six white-haired old ladies sat at banks of telephones facing the
windows, all engaged in whatever scheme that Lorna and Lucky were
currently promoting.

Lucky had on his black Stetson and, when he finally spotted me
hovering in the doorway, he doffed it in comic gallantry, waving it with
an absurd flourish and exposing his graying mess of thinning, straw-
colored hair.

"Well, if it isn't Miss Connie Eustace McQueen. It has been far
too long, young lady, since we were last graced with yer charming
presence."

The two girls at the table glared at me with dead rattlesnake
eyes. When I didn't say anything, Lucky chimed in again.

"You've caught us in a bit of a slowdown right now, Connie.
I know Lorna wanted to see you about augmenting one of our…" he
paused, searching for a euphemism, "…one of our one-off money-
making ventures. Temporary work that's easy as pie."

I thought to myself, "How the fuck is pie easy?"

"She's upstairs in her office. She's got somebody in with her
at the moment, but they'll be departing shortly. You should go on and
check in with her secretary."

When I turned round to head up the staircase, he called to me.

"Connie! Here, girl, this is for you. A little gift. A token of my
esteem."

He advanced a couple of steps and handed me one of the CDs.

"It's a remastering of all my golden oldies, all together, for the
first time!"

A trifle embarrassed, I took it from him, and he creepily let his
hand linger, caressing the palm of my hand with one long, bony
forefinger. I shivered and pulled away.

"Well, thanks, Lucky, that sure is mighty white of you."

I smiled, and his grin drooped. Before he had a chance to say anything else, I was off like a shot, taking the steps two at a time.

Why was I so scared of these people? They were a bunch of fools. When I got to the top of the steps, my jaunty self-confidence slipped down a peg.

I remembered certain things.

Acting the fool was their camouflage, especially with Lucky.

I greeted the young secretarial buck in a plaid cowboy shirt – he was good-looking in an airheaded kind-of-way and was undoubtedly on call to do double duty with Lorna in the sack. I told him my business, and he asked me to sit, saying Lorna would be done in a few minutes.

I plopped down in an antique armchair and scanned the song listings on the back of Lucky's CD:

"Fill 'Er Up, Girl, My Heart's on Empty"

"Tiny Boots Beside the Cradle" (his mournful ode to sudden crib death syndrome)

"Yer Pappy's Got a Hole in Him" (a tale of homicidal woe concerning a young stud going after the elderly man who has barred him from courting his 12-year-old daughter)

"Drowning in the Drunk Tank"

"Golden Nuts Upon My Horns" (a cuckold's revenge)

"Sadly Twisting, Oh, So Slowly in the Wind" (this had been his anti-capital punishment song, but when there'd been a public outcry from his largely conservative fanbase, he'd performed a sleight-of-hand, proclaiming it really was a pro-death penalty ditty; the lyrics are so nebulous, they believed him)

"SOBs Always Get Off Easy"

"Smilin' in the Morning's Got Me Cryin' till Late at Night"

"Car Wreck of a Heart"

"Open Up the Freezer Door Before My Cold Heart Cracks"

"I'm a Hit Parade Hitman Gonna Bust a Cap into your Top Ten"
(he'd been freebasing with some black rappers in Atlanta shortly before
writing these priceless lyrics)

"Don't Cook Me Turkey If I'm Nothin' but a Sittin' Duck to You"
(originally released a couple of weeks before one now long past
Thanksgiving holiday)

Plus there were these popular evergreen covers given the inimitable,
one-of-a-kind Lucky Fordyce treatment:

"Drop Kick Me, Jesus"

"I'm Drinkin' Christmas Dinner (All Alone This Year)"

"If I'd Killed You When I Wanted To, I'd be Out of Jail by Now"

"Mama Fetch the Hammer, There's a Fly on Papa's Head"

I'm a movie fanatic, so maybe this next bit here won't make much
sense to you – you might not know who I'm talking about. But, if you
can, just imagine teen sex bomb Carroll Baker in *Baby Doll*, add thirty-
five years to her age, then cross her with Jo Van Fleet in *East of Eden*
and Joan Crawford in *Queen Bee*, and you've got a pretty close picture
of what Lorna was like. A domineering but attractive woman, strikingly
handsome with long blonde hair, meticulously styled and coiffed. She
could veer from sweet and charming to poisonously vitriolic in a matter
of seconds. On rare occasions, if she was around her own sex, someone
she'd known a good while, she could show a surprising vulnerability.
At the same time, this vulnerability would be tinged with bitterness and
self-loathing. There was a mysterious power she had, a charisma, that
kept people working with her, even when things seemed to be going
downhill as far as her relationship and friendliness to that person. I
guess you could say I knew her pretty well, almost as well as Ray did.
But how can you ever really, truly know anybody?
        Right then the door to her office finally opened, and Mayor J.
Calden Jimsen materialized, sweating profusely in a lightweight, beige
summer suit. He was startled to see me, no doubt recalling the last
time we'd crossed paths, when I'd walked into the Maple Street house
to find him serving as the cream cheese center in a Jeannie and Janine

brown bread sandwich. He'd suggested at the time that we make it a quadruple decker, and I'd shut him down cold. He nodded to me, withdrew his handkerchief and mopped his bald head as he practically plummeted down the stairs.

I thought I could go in at that point, but another someone emerged, leaving the door open without a backwards glance to Lorna. I didn't know who he was at the time, but he was one of the most hideous bastards I've ever laid eyes on. A human abomination. Maybe 5'8" tops, his "physique" wasn't bad if you liked tightly-packed, stick-up-their-ass bodybuilder types. He had on a purple cotton cowboy shirt straining at the seams from his cartoonish muscle bulges, the long sleeves torn off at the shoulders to reveal a *USMC Semper Fi* tattooed on one inner forearm. Raggedy blue jeans hung over combat boots. Though it was what was perched on top of his shoulders as an excuse for a head that really gave new meaning to the word ugly: a peeled, upside-down hardboiled egg, both in consistency and shape – you know, the narrowest part at the bottom? – with a curly, scraggly mullet-style thatch of light brown hair on top. His eyebrows looked like they'd been scorched off. He couldn't have been more than 25 at the oldest. His teeth were obscenely bucked, and he had no chin to speak of, just a neck that kind of disappeared into the top of his chest in a concave slope, interrupted by an apricot pit-size Adam's apple that made my gorge rise. His nostrils were wide, and they flared outwards, near as bad as Lon Chaney in the original *Phantom of the Opera*. But what gave me the shudders were his black, shiny ball-bearing eyes, lighting up in their swampy depths when they fell on me. He grinned.

"Why, helloo-o-o-. You must be Connie. Your sexy reputation precedes you, girl."

Luckily, Lorna interrupted.

"Connie? C'mon in here, hon.' I got to talk to you."

I edged past the creature. He stood there gaping after me as I shut the door in his face.

"How the hell did that repulsive bastard know my name?"

"How the fuck should I know?"

I sat down in front of Lorna's immense mahogany desk, a Civil War antique that she'd inherited from Rolo. She looked stunning as usual, clad in tight-fitting white denim jacket and white jeans. Her tanned skin had the quality of burnished leather.

"I hope he's just passing through. Who is he?"

"It's none of yer business. But I guess there's no harm in telling. His name's Eli. And he *will be* around for a while. Just blew in from El Paso. Poor kid. His dad, Red, passed away a few months ago. Jeez, ole Red. Helluva crazy guy. Someone I did business with on occasion. I got a lot of fond memories of Red. A stand-up fella who knew the dog-race racket inside out."

"Why'd his kid have to land here? There's something wrong about him."

"You are just a big mess of insufferable curiosity today, ain't you?" She sighed. "He's investing in a little business venture I'm getting off the ground in the next month or two."

"Jimsen here to get in on the fix?"

"Connie, shut yer trap. You think 'cause your Ray's fiancée you can shoot yer mouth off any way you goddamn well please?"

"Yes."

"He's gonna tan yer hide once he gets back. If I don't do it first."

"What makes you think he's coming back? It's been months. You heard from him?"

She rose, bristling, and went over to the double doors that opened onto a rusty, wrought-iron balcony. "Fuck. 10:00 AM, and it's like a blast furnace already." She threw a troubled glance at me as she headed to the wet bar. She held up a fifth of gin in one hand, a quart of tonic in the other and looked at me questioningly. I nodded.

Once she was back at the desk, and we both had gin and tonics with plenty of ice, she started in again.

"Ray'll be back. If anything bad happened to him, anything really bad, I'd know. I ain't worried."

"Just have a feeling, hunh?"

She nodded. "And meanwhile, you can do me a favor. An errand. You should get out of town for a while, too…until Van Heusen cools down."

"Ernie and Fitz?"

She nodded.

"I didn't have anything to do with that."

"He knows you didn't. But he thinks you might have been a witness. For whatever-the-hell reason."

I just stared at her. We both sipped on our drinks.

"What's the errand?

"I need you to deliver a little something to one of my associates in New Orleans."

"Why me?"

"Goddamn it, Connie. Stop with the goddamn questions.

'Cause yer one of the only persons I can trust not to rip me off."

"Who's the associate?"

"Will you do it?"

"Who is it? I'm not particularly fond of your friends down there."

"You don't have much choice at this point."

"I don't, hunh?"

She slowly shook her head.

"You still haven't told me."

"Mr. Raindrop."

I knew it. "You mean Ennis Lacey?"

She looked fit to be tied. "Who told you his Christian name?"

"Ray. A long time ago. And there's nothing Christian about it. I know all about Ennis Lacey."

"I should've known."

"Ray and I don't have any secrets, Lorna. You know that."

"As far as yer concerned, Ennis Lacey's dead. The name of the man you need to meet is Mr. Raindrop."

I didn't say anything more, but she knew I was not happy.

"I need you to leave tonight. And, as I said, it's probably just as well you keep a low profile anyway."

Right then one of the lines on her phone buzzed and flashed. She picked up, staring at me the whole time. "Unh, hunh. I see. Put him on, Rich." She put her palm over the mouthpiece. "Connie, honey, I gotta take this. It's him. Wait a minute out there with Rich, will you?"

I did as she asked.

Mr. Raindrop. Give me a fucking break.

A few minutes later, she buzzed Rich, then he ushered me back to the inner sanctum.

"Okay. Change of plans. You still go, but not till next week. He's out of town until next Tuesday."

I frowned.

She knew I was doing the slow burn, and she didn't want to hear any sass. "Don't say it."

"What? Did I open my fuckin' mouth?"

"I got another favor you can do me…"

"Do I get anything out of all this?"

She started to get red in the face. "One day, yer gonna –"

"All right, Lorna. Forget it. What's the other favor?"

"You still working for me down at the Milk Train?

"Am I?"

"I'm overlookin' what happened to the hillbillies last night.
I know 'em, and they're assholes. They got what they deserved. I wish
I'd been there to see it." She took a deep breath. "The only two really
reliable girls I got down there are you and Janine. You both drink too
much, but I can trust you. Brenda, Carla and Lawanda are little thievin'
bitches and call in sick too often. They don't know it, but they're on the
way out as soon as I can find trustworthy replacements."

"What about Jeannie? Call her."

"You gotta be kiddin' me, girl."

"She has kind of gone off her rocker, hasn't she? But you got
her turnin' tricks over at the roadhouse, right?"

She took a long gulp on her drink, then used the back of one
hand to wipe her mouth as she studied me. "Who told you any of the
girls at Sleepy Eyes are turning tricks?"

"Just an educated guess."

She looked at me like she didn't believe me.

I was getting mad again. Did she think I was a complete
moron?

"Lorna, you got those Sleepy Eyes girls waiting on tables and
the bar in those teensy-weensy, baby doll, see-through nighties. With
nothing on underneath except thong panties!"

She gave me her icy stare, then to punctuate the coldness
emanating from her, clinked the ice cubes together in her almost empty
class. "Connie, you are drivin' me to distraction. And as far as Jeannie
goes, I fired her a couple of nights ago. I found out from the doctor, the
one I got the girls going to, she's got the AIDS."

I was too shocked to say anything.

"Don't look so surprised. None of those guys out there use
rubbers. There's not much I can do about it now, but I ain't havin' her
spreadin' that fag plague any further."

"You're probably a little late for that. Did the doctor tell
Jeannie?"

"Yeah. In fact, he told me that Jeannie begged him six ways
from Sunday not to tell me. Now honestly, how can the girl have
expected him to do that? I supply half his business."

"So, the good news just keeps on comin.' You might as well top
it off and tell me this other favor. Something about the Milk Train?"

She nodded. "You can take tonight off. But you work Thursday,
Friday and Saturday."

"What happened to me layin' low?"

"You do lay low when yer not at the club. Don't go out. Stay at fuckin' home. Or stay out here with me if you want. We both know Brody Van Heusen won't be caught dead walking into either The Milk Train or Sleepy Eyes because of his three bosom buddies from the New Testament: Jesus, Mary and Joseph."

"Yeah. I forgot. Half-naked bodies and whores are hell bait. Takin' payoffs from you and blowin' away soul brothers from 15 feet away, when all they got is a knife, perfectly acceptable."

She ignored my sarcasm. "Sonny Jessup has a crush on you and will look the other way, regardless of whether Brody wants him to bring you in."

"Both of them are on your payroll anyway, right, Lorna?"

She ignored my jibe and answered me with a question. "Well? You in or out on this? I mean, doin' me the favors?"

"I haven't got much choice. As you so considerately pointed out. But I'm going to ask you a favor, too. If I agree."

"What?"

"I want to leave on Sunday morning and take one of your cars. I can stop over a couple nights in Hattiesburg and visit my Aunt Vivian. It's not too far out of the way. Then Tuesday AM I head into New Orleans."

She hesitated before consenting, trying to see my angle and if there was a way I could somehow screw her.

Finally, she nodded. "All right."

I chugged the rest of my drink.

Downstairs, when I was leaving, sitting waiting outside on the porch for Janine to pick me up, I saw a strange sight. Crazy Lester, the drunken, snake-handling preacher – *Wiseblood*'s Hazel Motes on crack – was strolling with Lucky Fordyce along the side of the big dilapidated house. They appeared deep in conversation. Lester had his head bowed in an uncharacteristic pose of reflection, his hands clasped behind his back and his wide brimmed hat pulled low, casting a shadow over his unshaven face. Lucky had his right hand poised thoughtfully up to his cheek, his long, lecherous index finger rubbing the side of his nose. Unless I missed my guess, they were discussing scripture. Seeing them both like that, engaged in "philosophical discourse," would prove to have disturbing reverberations not too much further down the road.

Chapter 15

When I got home I was tired and despondent, so I weaved wearily to my room and crawled into the small double bed, a full fifth of Jack Daniels and six pack of Dixie keeping me company on the floor. I stacked Wilson, James, Otis, with Al Green at the top, on the record changer of my broken-down stereo and turned up the volume. Janine had gone back out. When my drunk got its angry on, I switched the records to the Stones, the Sonics, the Stooges and the Saints. Somebody from the next door neighbor's yard started yelling "shut up" when Iggy launched into *Your Pretty Face is Going to Hell*. I ignored them. Fuck her. It was fat-ass Addie Troy.

I was still alone at midnight, just drinking, feeling sorry for myself and dwelling on thoughts of Ray. I had a couple lamps, one on either side of the bed. My reading light on the old mahogany bedstead was plain, but the ones on the nightstands had blue bulbs. They fit perfectly with my mood that night. My depression deepened as the hours wore on. I only got up to change records.

Whenever I happen to hit the absolute rock bottom of the pit, I put on old country, this time Hank Williams, Porter Wagoner, Patsy Cline and really early Loretta Lynn. Just as Porter began *The Cold Hard Facts of Life,* Janine poked in her head.

I turned the volume down a little.

"I know you gotta be in bad shape listening to that shit."

"Fuck you."

"To each her own."

She settled her voluptuous ass on the edge of the bed.

"What did Lorna want?"

I could barely talk. I explained about my planned rendezvous in New Orleans with the debonair Mr. Raindrop.

"Shee-it, honey. I don't like the sound of this. That's Ennis Lacey's alias now, right?"

"Why do you think I'm drinking."

"You never needed an excuse before." She grabbed the fifth that was three quarters gone and upended it, sucking up a healthy jolt. "So, why do you feel obligated to do this for her?"

"Because she's Ray's mama."

"You need your head examined. You keep going back and forth between being a take-no-prisoners hard-ass and a milquetoast pushover."

I took the bottle away from her. "My inferiority complex and mother issues have got me between rock and a hard place," I slurred.

Janine grimaced. "Remind me before you go. I've got a couple names I'll give you, good people you can call if something freaky goes down."

She crawled up onto the bed beside me and folded her arms around my waist from behind.

Janine holds a special place in my heart. I'm not sure why. She and Jeannie lost their mother at the same age as me, from heart disease. Their father was already in Angola, and they never saw him again. We met at around that same time, actually about a year before, in high school. She often kids me about my having more education – they dropped out of school after 10th grade, and she pokes fun at some of the words I use, my vocabulary. I guess it's a strange kinship that she and I have developed. It never clicked with me and Jeannie, and Jeannie's been jealous of the two of us ever since.

We lay there spooning like that till the song was over. I was so drunk, I don't remember much else, except, at some point, I seem to recall rolling over and pulling down her top, letting lose her fabulous tits. She cradled me to her, and I sucked at her breasts like a newborn.

When I awoke the next mid-afternoon, I had a king-size hangover and, as night approached, I knew there was no way on earth I could stand

upright on that stage at the Milk Train for more than a minute or two at
a stretch. So, I stayed in bed, knowing more than likely I would incur
Lorna's wrath.

And I did. She called me early the following morning.

"Is this the way you keep your word?" She was shouting and
hot.

I fumbled towards a coherent train of thought. "I was sick last
night."

"Too drunk you mean."

"That, too."

"You're not there tonight, just see what happens," she
threatened, then slammed the receiver down in my ear.

Why was she so anxious to get me at the club, to see me up on
that stage those nights? Her complaint about a shortage of reliable girls,
dancers, didn't wash. My paranoia blossomed, and the seed of some
unknown dread started to grow in my stomach. It worsened as the hours
ticked by, akin to the worst menstrual cramps imaginable, and it started
me drinking again. I took a couple Xanax. That helped a little.

I drove in with Janine. She knew I was fearful, and she was a champion
handholder.

We got there around 7:30 because she wanted to eat a little
something while the kitchen was still open. Me, I couldn't have kept
anything down on a bet. As the night grew old, I foolishly kept
drinking. Each of us girls – generally five a night – do five ten minute
shifts each hour, with a ten minute break at the end before each 60
minute slot runs out. There are five of those hour shifts. Everything
in fives. By the fourth, I was overcome with a sucking, caved-in heart
depression. It was around 11, and otherwise I was feeling no physical
pain. My inhibitions were thrown out the window even more than
usual. Despair overwhelmed me, and I was determined to escape
through acting out.

I usually don't get too radical with my act's music, because
some of the old-school boys who come in just can't take it. But, for the
next song, I had the DJ spin a 45 I'd brought from home, a bootleg of
Iggy and the Stooges' *Cock in My Pocket*. I got nasty during the tune,
not just losing my top, but pouring beer all over my tits, then hefting
them up to lick the liquor off the nipples. The place was only a third
full, and it went wild. Halfway through the song I did something I'd
never done before – at least onstage. You have to understand, despite
the payoffs to law officers and the illustrious court of Mystic, we still

could not get away with fully exposing our asses or pussies. That night, I didn't care. I smashed against the pillars on stage, bumping and grinding. I went to the lip of the stage, thrusting out my pelvis, one hand waving in the air, twirling my bra, the other hand suddenly thrust down my panties, wildly finger-fucking myself like there was no tomorrow. Some of the audience went stone quiet, their mouths gaping open. Other boys and men increased their volume, their whooping and hollering more than making up for the others' shocked silence.

And then I saw him, near the back.

Ray.

His face didn't register with me at first because I was so damn drunk. His expression was corpse-like, ashen. He was ghostly pale, and I was sure he'd lost some weight. His appearance had something to do with how long it took me to really see it was him. When the song was on the last couple of bars, I finally recognized his eyes. Maybe it was my own shame and insecurity, but there was a horrible expression of disgust and loathing etched on his features. Then he was gone.

Before the last guitar chord had faded, I'd jumped off the stage, feverishly repositioning and fastening my bra as I ran through the stunned crowd. I knocked over a table near the entrance as I pushed between the twin behemoths of Mort and Lee.

"Get yer goddamn fat asses out of my way!"

They both tried to grab me, but I was too slick from beer and baby oil, and the next thing I knew I was doing laps around the dirt lot, my eyes darting everywhere trying to catch a trace of Ray. He was gone.

Lee followed me. "Connie, if you lookin' for Ray, he hightailed it in his car." He laughed, rubbing it in with relish. "Peeled out of here like a bat out of hell."

I stood there, all the way across the lot from him, my mascara and make-up running down my cheeks as tears started to come.

"Come on back in here, girl. You got another set to do."

I sank to my knees, sobbing.

He waved his hand at me in disgust, wheeled his fat gut around and disappeared back inside the club. Any minute I knew there'd be guys coming out into the lot. I picked myself up and ran into the trees that skirted the parking area. They got thicker the further I ran. My heels got stuck in the roots of some huge oak, and I went flying, smashing into the dead leaves that blanketed the uneven ground. I lay there for I don't know how long, weeping.

I hadn't really been paying attention before, but the sweltering humidity suddenly seemed like an oppressive blanket thrown over me.

Sometime later, I felt a gentle hand on my shoulder. It was Janine. She had my leather jacket with her, and she slipped my arms into it as she hoisted me up, treating me like a mother would treat her long lost child. She wiped the dirt and pieces of leaves from my face with a handkerchief, hugged me tight for a few seconds, then led me out of the woods, one arm draped protectively over my shoulder.

Returning to the lot, I saw that only Janine's GTO and a couple other employees' vehicles remained. It was after closing time. Once we were in her car, I regained my power of speech.

"You see him?"

"Ray? No, but I heard from Brenda and Mort that he was there. Fucking weird. Why didn't he come by the house earlier? Or try to call? I don't get it."

Then I knew with a chilling certainty – that's why Lorna wanted to make sure I was there onstage, doing my thing *those* nights.

Chapter 16

Next thing I knew we were at the house, Janine steering me as I tottered through the front door, then into my cluttered bedroom. I plopped on the unmade mattress. I hadn't had any hard liquor since about 10 and no beer since 11. When I looked at the clock, I was astonished to see it was past 4 AM. Time flew when you were having so much fun. And I was virtually sober, compared to earlier in the evening.

Janine strutted in, took out a tiny, folded piece of paper and emptied its white powder contents on the mirror top of my low-slung chest of drawers. She chopped it into lines, rolled up a dollar bill, then quickly snorted a couple, wincing, coughing and squeezing her prominent, aquiline nostrils together between thumb and forefinger.

She looked at me.

I shook my head like a spoiled brat. "I don't want any fucking coke."

"It's not coke, honey."

"Crank'd be even worse. I need to get down, not up. Down and out."

"I know, I know, baby girl. This is smack."

I looked at her dumbly.

"Not sure if I should give you any, though. You were so damn drunk earlier. Liquor and junk don't mix well."

"I've had it before." Though it had been a couple of years, and the little I'd done that time had made me sick.

"How you feel?"

"Not drunk, if that's what you mean."

She bent over me, placing her hands on either side of my temples, then used her thumbs and forefingers to pry my eyelids wide open. She turned my head towards the meager blue light on the nearest nightstand, trying to examine my pupils.

"This stuff is strong. I'll let you do half a line to start. See how you do."

She stood beside me as I got up and bent over the dresser. She put one arm affectionately around my shoulders as she handed me the dollar bill. She chopped away at a line till it was evenly cut in two.

"Just half now, Connie. I mean it."

I followed her instructions. It hit me quickly, and I nearly keeled over from the swooning rush. At that point, I'd never shot it, so I could only imagine how spectacular it must be. But my euphoria was short-lived as the aftertaste of whatever the dealer had used to cut it made me gag.

Janine slammed open the window beside the bed and whirled me round to face it. I stumbled to the sill, propping my hands on the dusty wood. I stuck out my head, seeing the tangled overgrown garden in our backyard, spectral in the moonlight. But I didn't throw up.

When the nausea passed, the euphoria returned, though not on as intense a level. I seemed to float back to the bed. Again, I noticed how fucking hot it still was, the stifling wetness of the air around me, making me feel almost as if I was underwater. I was sweating heavily, and it seemed like every inanimate object in the room was sweating along with me.

Ray. Where was Ray? My pulsating need to find him after he'd run off had diminished from a sharp, unendurable pang ripping out my guts to a dull, bearable ache. When I awoke, I would look for him. I'd comb the entire town. I'd get up early, and I'd find him. No matter how long it took. But, even though the morning was already all around me, for all intents and purposes, my floating on a delicious pink cloud told me not to worry about it till tomorrow. When the sun was up.

When I finally opened my eyes, I was face-down on the dirty Persian carpet beside my bed. I'd drooled on the rug, and my mouth felt like it was filled with acidic cotton. I tried to push up from that prone position, but couldn't do it. It took several attempts before I was able.

Finally, I made it to a kneeling position. I must have still been a little
high, because I didn't feel too bad. Then a wave of nausea washed over
me. I lurched to the open window and poked my head out into the
sunlight. There on the ground outside the window was a splatter of
puke, confirming what the taste in my mouth told me. At some point,
I had gotten sick. Then I noticed something that made tears well up
and drive the nausea away. A newly dead sparrow lay beside the vomit
in the dirt. Had it been hungry, mistakenly thinking it discerned some
nourishment in my heaved-up toxins? If so, had ingesting those
indigestible morsels of poison fatally polluted the poor little critter's
innards?

I pulled my head back in and looked at the alarm clock. It was
10 AM.

I needed to start looking for Ray.

I didn't know how long I was going to hold up before I folded
again, what with the abuse I'd put myself through the night before. But
I wasn't thinking about that, let alone that I had to perform again that
night, per my promise to Lorna. Then again, the obvious reason Lorna
had wanted me onstage – to show the returned-from-oblivion Ray what
a worthless slut I was – cancelled my obligations to her.

I had it fixed in my mind that I just had to find Ray as soon as
possible. Otherwise I felt I might cave and show up at the club on the
slim chance he'd have second thoughts and come looking for me.

Janine was passed out on the couch with the TV on at low
volume. I shook her gently. She surfaced slowly from whatever depths
she'd been swimming in.

"What's up? What you doin' up so early?"

"Let me borrow your car."

"To look for Ray?"

I nodded.

She sighed. "I guess nothing I'd say would stop you."

"Why should you stop me?"

"No reason, I guess. I just think he'll find you when he's cooled
down."

"Well, if by some miracle I have a change of heart, I'm still
supposed to honor my promise to his cunt of a mother and head to the
club tonight and to New Orleans tomorrow."

"Fuck. I forgot. All right." She grabbed the keys from the
coffee table and thrust them up at me. "Just try to stay clear of Van
Heusen."

"You don't have to remind me."

I still had on my club outfit from the night before, so I pulled on a blouse and tiny skirt before I left the house. As I opened the door, I looked back at Janine. "Thanks."

Only her hand appeared above the top of the couch, waving in acknowledgment.

The heat had broken a bit, but the air was still thick with a clingy moisture that gradually wore away at my initial enthusiasm to go on the hunt.

Wearing wraparound shades, I poised low in the GTO's seats, keeping a lookout for law. I hit Jake's garage first, a place where Ray had often worked and hung out, but it was closed. Jake lived on the second floor, but I couldn't raise him, no matter how hard I knocked.

Next I stopped at Moe's Country Style Diner. Moe is a gal, not a guy, and she's never been overly fond of Ray or me. But we'd often eaten there in the past because it was one of the few restaurants in Mystic where the food was edible.

There were only a couple of booths filled, one with an old couple, each with one foot in the grave, and the other a picture-postcard family that looked like they'd just been to church. Strange, because it was Saturday.

Moe was not happy to see me. I sat down at the counter, but she continued to bat flies with her swatter as if she hadn't noticed. At last, I waved. She wearily dropped the swatter under the counter and shuffled over. She was a year or two past sixty, but looked older, and her hideous yellow-grey wig gleamed in the sunlight coming through the front window. She was tough – the kind who ate nails for breakfast.

"Hoped I'd seen the last of you two."

"Why? You see Ray today?"

"Don't tell me you don't know? Thought you two good-for-nothings were inseparable. I was actually surprised you weren't with him."

"What time was he in?"

She put one hand on her hip and stared at me, trying to decide if she was going to really condescend to having a conversation.

"6 AM. Crack of dawn, just after I opened. He didn't look any too good. And he was his usual friendly self."

"You can cut the sarcasm."

"I can cut conversation with you, period, girl."

I swallowed my pride. "Sorry."

"You gonna order something?"

I didn't feel like it, but... "Coffee."

She poured a cup and plopped it down in front of me so some of it sloshed onto the counter.

"Well, he ordered a huge breakfast. Ham and eggs and grits and mounds of toast, a pot of coffee and a couple of glasses of orange juice. But then when I brought it to him, he just looked at it. He couldn't eat it. Said he'd lost his appetite. He wouldn't say so, but I could tell something was gnawing at his guts. I said, 'You look like you got somethin' heavy weighin' on your mind.'" She snorted with derision. "That set him off. He goes, 'I didn't come in here to get psycho-analyzed.' The nerve! You better tell that boyfriend –"

"What else he say?"

"He didn't say anything. But he knocked all his food and drink on the floor. Lucky Herbie wasn't here, or there would've been blood-shed. I was so shocked, I couldn't say a word. Then he suddenly starts apologizin', saying he'll pay twice the amount he owes and whatever damages. He plunked down a fifty dollar bill on the counter, and I shouted at him to get the hell out before I called the law. He looked at me strange, like I hurt his feelin's. Then he was gone."

"Did you see what he was driving? Which way he went?"

She shook her head in disgust. "I wasn't payin' much attention, seein' how I was cleanin' up the godawful mess he left behind."

I took a couple of swallows of the coffee. It was scalding but good and strong as usual. "How much I owe?"

"A dollar."

I fished out two and left them on the counter.

The most likely place to find him, I didn't want to go. But I didn't have a choice. I was like a jonesing junkie who'd just been handed a full rig, then was told not to fix.

I didn't want to go to Lorna's for a couple of reasons. Afraid that he'd be there, and he'd refuse to see me – for whatever mysterious motive – or he wouldn't be there, and then Lorna would tell me various lies and half-truths till I couldn't tell which end was up.

When I pulled in front of the house, I didn't see any unfamiliar cars parked, just the regulars.

I had to run more of a gauntlet than usual. The beehive bouffant girls who had their asses perpetually welded to the chairs in the big front room gave me a dose of grief. A lot of it.

"Lorna ain't seein' nobody at the moment, darlin'. She had a bit too much to drink last night, and's a bit, well you know, under the weather?"

The way she said that last part like a question made me want to smash her face in. "I'm not askin' to see her. I'm tellin'."

"That so?" The one with the puffier hairdo and the dark mascara and the deep-set eyes, stood up, hands on her hips.

I nodded and took a step towards her, mimicking her pose.

She got extra snotty. "You ain't tellin' nobody nothin'. Nobody died and made you queen. Yer just a pathetic lil' piece of white trash sniffin' around for the crumbs Lorna and Ray leave after their meal."

I grabbed her by her hair with one hand, wrapping the cotton candy-like substance around my fist, and with my other, twisted her right arm behind her back.

"Listen you piss-stained whore, nobody gets away with talkin' trash like that to me." I brought my mouth close to her ear and whispered, "Nobody! Especially a smelly little twat like you!"

"Bea, honey. It's okay." It was Lorna's voice coming from behind me. "Connie, please let Beatrice go. I won't ask you to apologize, 'cause I'm sure you won't. But I will ask you, as a special favor to me, not to treat my employees that way in the future."

I let the girl go, and she fell on the floor, clumsily catching herself before she went all the way down, pushing up with one hand to twist herself away to land and hide behind her open-mouthed sister.

Lorna had a tired expression on her face, like she'd been up all night. She didn't say a word, just wagged her head towards the staircase as she climbed up, expecting me to follow.

She wearily closed the office door behind us and pointed to the purple-velvet sofa by the French windows. I sat down on one end, and she stationed herself at the other.

"What brings you out so early on a Saturday?"

"Please, Lorna. Don't play games with me. Not about this. You know why."

"Do I?"

Was she trying to push my fucking buttons? She must have been. She knew that I knew that she knew Ray was in town. She had to, even if Ray hadn't gotten in touch with her – which I sincerely doubted. One of her Milk Train people would have certainly let her know. They talked to her on the phone, giving her the take, every damn night right after closing.

"You know I know, Lorna. Even if Ray didn't call you. Mort or Lee or one of your other goddamn lapdogs at the club would have mentioned it."

She didn't want to talk. She looked away for a few seconds then, bracing herself, dove right in.

"He showed up last night, around eight. No call, no warnin', nothin.' Just showed up." She was getting pale around the gills as she told it. "He looked like death warmed over. He wouldn't say much. Except that he'd been to hell and back. Literally, to hear him tell it. He wouldn't go into details. Said that could wait till later. I know he got into some real serious trouble. That's why he was gone so long. Anyway…he wanted to know if it was true that you were workin' for me. You know, strippin' out at The Milk Train. I didn't know what to tell him."

"Really? Are you sure him being in town isn't the reason you wanted to make sure I showed up onstage the last couple of nights?"

"What? To cause a rift between you two?"

"You are priceless."

"I don' like what yer insinuatin', Connie. This is serious. I don't toy around with people's emotions like that. Especially not kin. Most ways, I've already considered you Ray's wife. I'd never want to cause heartache between you two."

I couldn't tell if she was lying or not. There were plenty of times when she'd gone out of her way to look out for me while Ray was gone. She was aware of the last time I'd spoken to Ray on the phone, about how conflicted I was about telling him what I'd been doing to make ends meet. And that I'd chickened out, not telling him anything.

"So what happened when he came by, unannounced? What'd he say?"

"I asked him, 'You go see Connie yet?' He says, 'No. I just got into town a couple of hours ago.'"

She paused, apparently afraid to tell me more.

"And…?"

"I said, 'I would've thought she'd be the first one you'd go see.'" She took a dramatic deep breath. "He – he was like a ghost, Connie. He got all white. He goes, 'I couldn't. Not yet. I need to know, Mama…she strippin' out at that shithole for you?' I just nodded, and he put his head in his hands, staring at the floor."

I got up and went to the bar. I poured a shot of Jack and tossed it down. For a few seconds, that heroin alcohol hangover seemed right on the verge of rearing its ugly head. I pounded another shot, feeling "What the fuck!" and the surge of nausea dwindled to a manageable level.

"Is he stayin' here, Lorna?" I turned to look her in the eyes, but she wouldn't meet my stare.

"No."

I paced briskly to the couch and knelt down on the cushions beside her. She slowly turned to face me.

"Lorna, I need for you to tell me the truth. He stayin' here or not?"

"No, I said. I don't know where he is. I told him whatever trouble he was in, I'd help him work it out. Somehow, some way, I'd make it right. He didn't seem to care one way or another."

I stood up. She kept on.

"Mort told me last night what happened with you an' Ray at the club. I know it ain't good."

"Lorna, you and I have known each other a long, long while. We haven't always seen eye to eye. But I've always respected you because you were Ray's mother. I know you didn't have an easy time of it before you married Rollo. I know you built up this little backwater empire from scratch after Rollo died, practically all by your lonesome. That takes guts and smarts and the ability to keep a lot of balls in the air. I know this town and how it works. You've made yourself pretty much the boss of this county. You're more the mayor of Mystic than Jimsen. That's all well and good. That's separate from you and Ray and me. Separate from the family part. I always felt you had some real affection for me. Maybe it was real, maybe it was just play-acting for Ray's sake. Whatever it's been, Lorna, I don't ever, ever want to come between you and Ray. You and your son. I know he's your only blood kin. All the same, I just hope to God you're tellin' me the truth."

She looked at me, not uttering a word for a good couple of minutes. At last, she came out with a bit of self-interest for which I should have been prepared. But I wasn't, because it had completely slipped my mind.

"Listen, Connie. I know it's gonna be harder than hell 'cause of whatever seems to be goin' on between you an' Ray. But I still need you to go to New Orleans for me tomorrow. I only trust you to do this. And now that Ray's back, it's more important than ever. Because at this point, if what I think has gone down with Ray is true, Mr. Raindrop is the only person on earth who can help him."

Lorna is a great actress. If she was in the movies, she could easily win an Oscar. My bullshit-detector was on full bore, but my bias of being obsessively in love with Ray was affecting my judgment. Was she telling me the truth? Was she lying to me? Or was she only telling me part of what was going on, leaving out stuff that would prevent her from getting me to do what she wanted?

I was so mixed up, so desperate and so angry, I was forgetting to eat. I was ignoring anything that didn't have to do with finding Ray. I didn't want to go to strip at the Milk Train that night but, as I'd feared, my antenna was fine-tuned to where Ray might turn up, and I was desperate enough to go down there. It was a slight chance, at best.

My memory of going home to get dressed for that night is virtually non-existent. Maybe because when I got to the club, the thing I recall, what I most vividly remember is what immediately greeted me in the parking lot. There was a two-tone 1980 Mustang parked away from the other regular employees' cars. It was kind of funky-looking what with its rough, unfinished primer, and I didn't think much about it till I got closer and recognized Ray's sullen profile, a cigarette with a hellaciously long cone of ash hanging on the end. A burning flush of fear and anticipation and confused excitement rushed through me as I walked up to the driver's side. He was preoccupied, unaware of me until I was nearly on top of him. When he finally turned to look up at my face, there was a visible tremor in his body, but he quickly got hold of himself. He couldn't hide his eyes, though, which were wet around the edges. At least I knew he cared. But what was eating him? Seeing me in that shameful display the night before? Or was there something else, even worse?

"Ray...I'm sorry I didn't tell you before."

He glared at me, not saying a word. He flicked the smoldering butt into the dirt and sparks flew as it hit.

"I had to do something to bring in some money, and Lorna offered me the job."

"Don't fuckin' blame Mama."

"I'm not blaming her. I knew you'd be unhappy if I told you, and there was no way I could bring myself to do it over the phone. I thought we'd see each other before you'd ever find out. And I could tell you then."

He glowered at me, refusing to speak.

"Well, you wouldn't've wanted to hear it over the phone, would you? I'm sorry about last night. I was drunk and stoned and in despair, mainly 'cause I didn't think I was ever gonna fuckin' see you again. You were gone, what? Three months longer than you said you'd be? Where were you? A hospital? Jail? I thought you might even be dead. And living in this goddamn sewer that just keeps getting worse and worse, waiting for you, not knowing how long it'd be…This town is…is…" I couldn't finish. My voice was starting to break up. I knew I was going to cry, and I didn't want to go there.

He turned his face away and started the car.

"What happened to you, Ray, honey? Can't you tell me?"

He let the car idle, and he stared straight ahead.

Early-bird patrons were starting to pull into the lot.

"Is there something else than what happened last night that's on your mind? You never called me again that whole time you were gone. You didn't call me when you got into town or try to come by. First time I know you're here is seeing you in the back of the club…"

He snuck a quick glance at me, then put the car into gear and steered out of the lot.

"Ray!" My throat constricted with a horrible sadness. I felt as if I couldn't breathe. Tears rolled down my cheeks.

"Well, if it isn't little Miss Muffett getting ready to sit on a tuffett, and eat 'er some curds and whey."

I turned to see that ugly monster, Eli, playing the corny asshole, exiting the club, loping towards me like a leering wolf.

"Lorna didn't tell you, I bet. But I'm the new manager at the Milk Train. Starting tonight. Can you beat that, girl? You an' me are gonna be working together."

When he got close enough, I spat in his face.

Before I knew what hit me, he struck, and I went down in the dirt. A couple of farmers from up the road stood slackjawed a few yards away, watching an uppity bitch get hers. I picked myself up to a sitting position in the swirling dust, rubbing the blood from my lips with the back of my hand.

"Why you monkey-lookin' cocksucker…"

He raised his booted leg to stomp me, but I drove my fist between his legs, landing a hard right to his balls. He let out an excruciated yelp, but still fell on me, his own hands chugging overtime, then turning me over on my stomach and pinioning me, twisting my left arm round my back till I felt something snap. Then there was Janine and Brenda and Eva jumping on him from behind, pulling him off me. He was going nuts. Luckily Sonny Jessup pulled into the lot right then and screeched to a halt beside us.

The pain in my arm was suddenly so bad I was blacking out. He'd broken it, sure.

When I came to a minute later, Sonny was helping me to my

feet. Janine, Brenda and Eva each stood with their arms folded, a yard or so behind the now sheepish-looking Eli.

"Looks like we had a little misunderstanding here…"

I cried out as Sonny touched my arm. He became genuinely concerned.

"Connie, honey, I think you went and got yourself a fracture."

I couldn't answer, but I could see Eli smirking over Sonny's shoulder.

"Well, y'all…is somebody gonna tell me what happened?"

I wheezed out my reply before anyone else. "I just had a little accident, trippin' in these damn heels." I winced at both the pain in my forearm and at covering for the mullet-headed rat. "Eli was very *courteously* helping me up."

"Didn't look that way to me." Sonny gave Eli a dirty look, then wagged his head at Janine. "You're her friend. That what happened?"

Janine glanced at me, and I nodded. She frowned, hating to tell a lie. "Yeah, Connie should know, I guess." She exhaled. "That's the way it happened."

"Hmm, when I pulled in here my eyes must've been playing tricks. I had a distinctly different impression." He stared at Eli. "Don't believe I've had the pleasure…"

Eli stuck out his hand, and Sonny reluctantly took it. "I'm the new manager here. Lorna Diamond hired me today. Name's Eli."

Sonny let go his hand and didn't answer him. He looked at me.

"Guess this employee of yours has got a night off. Probably more like a couple weeks off. I better get you to a doctor."

He escorted me to the other side of the cruiser, and gently sat me down in the front passenger seat. I sank my neck back against the top of the warm upholstery and closed my eyes as he started the car and coasted slowly out of the lot.

"You startin' a one-woman war, Connie?"

I didn't answer.

"I heard Ray's back. Surprised you two aren't hanging out together."

"Sonny, I can't think straight from how bad this hurts. I'd appreciate you postponing the third degree till another time."

He glanced at me, then shrugged, and we rode the rest of the way to the doctor in an uncomfortable silence.

Sonny stayed with me, stoic and comparatively quiet, while Doc Clayburn put a cast on my forearm. The fracture was what they call a "greenstick," meaning the bone was only partially cracked and not broken all the way through. Doc gave me some heavy duty codeine for the pain and plenty to take with me, enough to last a few days. Doc had once had a practice with my father, years gone by.

"Now, girl, I know yer a drinker. Be careful with these and don't over-indulge with the alcohol. An' keep to the prescribed dose, only one every four hours."

He winked and felt the cast, making sure it was all set.

When I told him how it had happened – while Sonny was out using the men's room – Doc insisted that he'd bill Lorna, and she could pass the financial hurt along to her new employee, if she saw fit.

I had Sonny drop me at Lorna's afterward. I told him not to wait.

Lorna wasn't happy to see me, being in that damaged condition.

"I guess you aren't goin' to be borrowin' one of my cars for yer trip. You can't drive like that. They're all stick."

Like I was an idiot. "Yeah, I figured. I'll take the bus to Hattiesburg. I called Aunt Vivian already. There's a bus pulling out in a few hours, around ten, I think. It'll get me there around 6 AM. I'll sleep the whole way."

"So you still set on going to Hattiesburg?"

I nodded. She didn't like it, but there wasn't much she could do. She knew I was on the verge of telling her to fuck off.

"Don't worry. I'll take the bus into New Orleans Monday night. Get there Tuesday morning, bright and early."

She took out a bundle of what was undoubtedly cash, wrapped and taped in several folds of newspaper. She threw it into my lap. "That's what yer takin' for Mr. Raindrop. Don't lose it."

I nodded. "You haven't asked me how I broke my arm, Lorna."

She stared at me for a few seconds before answering. "Your pal, Janine, called right after it happened, givin' me an earful about Eli. A whole week's ration of bullshit."

"That guy is crazy. What hold's he got on you? Something to do with Ray?"

Lorna swiveled in her chair and broke eye contact, focusing on the far corner of the room.

I kept prodding. "That's it, isn't it?"

She nodded. "It's a long story…which I'm not going to go into full-bore now. If you and Ray ever get on speaking terms again, you can have him tell you. It was a stupid stunt he pulled. And Eli's dad, Red, was a friend of mine. It's fucked up. And Eli's fucked up. I'm not happy dealin' with him. But he's in with Mr. Raindrop. Eli and Red and Mr. Raindrop – and the mob in Louisiana, Texas and New Mexico – all have a stake in this shit. At this point, I'm just tryin' to keep Ray from gettin' whacked."

I was shocked it was that bad.

"What the fuck Ray do to get a contract taken out on him?"

"He knocked over the wrong place in El Paso. One of the things that's happenin' now – if you must know – is that Mr. Raindrop's gettin' about half the money back, Eli another quarter, and they're both getting a piece of the pie in Mystic. What's been my whole pie up until now, except for a small percentage that's already been goin' to some folks in Atlanta and Macon."

"Sounds like too many cooks in the kitchen."

"You got that right."

"And I'm takin' Ennis Lacey, aka the magical Mr. Raindrop, his payoff?"

She nodded.

"It stinks."

"Did I say it didn't? It's the only game in town. So get used to it. That is if you still give a damn about Ray. I don't expect you to do it on my account."

Lorna had already wanted me to be her New Orleans courier *before* Ray was back. Which means she was lying one way or another. She'd already talked to him and, of course, to Eli.

I walked over to the French windows. The white lace curtains hung limp, like they were stunned by the muggy heat. Something curious caught my eye out in the yard. Lucky Fordyce was standing kind of forlorn by the old cypress tree, gazing at the ground. Suddenly he dropped to his knees and folded his hands together in an attitude of prayer.

I laughed softly. "Will wonders never cease?"

Curiosity getting the better of her, Lorna was soon standing by my side. There was an abrupt intake of her breath when it registered what Lucky was doing. By the time I turned to look at her, she'd regained her composure.

"What's wrong?"

"What isn't? Now I got that damn fool gettin' religion, right when I need his help most." She angrily spun on her heel and sat down again at her desk.

I shuffled over, my drug and alcohol fog kicking in. "I'm going to need some traveling money, Lorna. I know you don't want me opening this package of yours."

She pulled a thick stack of bills out of nowhere, peeling off five fifties and fifteen twenties. "Here. Call me tomorrow from Hattiesburg."

I nodded, took the cash and left.

Out in the yard, I veered around the side of the house in a daze. Lucky was startled when I pulled him up by the shoulder.

"Just the man I want to see."

He was surprised at my cast. "What happened to you?"

"A bulldozer ran into my outhouse. Don't ask me fool questions. I need a ride home. You're elected."

Chapter 17

Lucky frowned as he was driving, something heavy clouding his normally sunny horizon.

"Didn't know you were the religious type, Lucky. What were you doin' prayin' out by that tree?"

He glanced at me. "Connie, I look on you as an awfully attractive girl. And an awfully smart one. Which means you should have already guessed, the less you know about anything goin' on at that house, the better."

I felt like pushing it. "You still haven't answered my question."

"You really are stubborn. Just like yer pa. Bet you didn't know I knew him, long time ago before that horrible accident."

"I don't give a damn if you knew him or not."

He sighed. "You insist on knowin' what I was doin,' I was prayin' for a dearly departed soul."

"Who?"

"Yer not goin' to get that out of me, girl, so you better stop tryin'."

He pulled up in front of my house and let the engine idle as he turned to face me.

"If you live to be as old as me, Connie, you'll undoubtedly have a few things weighin' heavy on yer mind. Things you did when you were younger – even a few years younger – that you might not be so proud of anymore."

He looked away out the windshield, watching as Addie Troy's backward little boy drove his bicycle in circles in the middle of the road. He fished in his top pocket for a cigarette, took one, propped it between his liverish lips and lit up.

"Anyway…you better get on in the house, honey. An' stop mindin' other people's business."

I frowned, awkwardly opened the door and climbed out. He leaned over to look at me.

"You take care of yourself, sugar. New Orleans can be a rough town. Especially Mr. Raindrop's crowd."

He stretched out one arm, pulled the door shut, then sped away, nearly hitting the boy on the bike.

It was getting closer to the time I needed to leave, and it didn't look like I was going to get a ride to the bus. What with my broken arm, I wasn't sure how much I should try to take with me. Despite the codeine, the whole limb was pulsating with a dull ache. I was staring down at my backpack, wondering if I could survive a couple days with just one change of clothes, when I heard the front screen door open, then slam.

"You home?" It was Janine. She practically danced into the room, stoned on weed. Her eyes went wide as she caught sight of the cast.

"Jesus, it really did get broken."

I gave her a dirty look. "How'd you get away from the club, what with that slimy egghead of a prick callin' the shots now?"

"Fuck that frog-headed little rat. I told him I had to go home for half an hour to see how you were."

"Good timing. You can drop me at the bus stop."

"Shoot, that's right. Can't drive stick with an arm like that. You still stoppin' in Hattiesburg?"

"Already called Aunt Viv. She'll have her new hubby drive over to the station to pick me up."

I stuffed a halter top, a sweater, a couple of skirts, a pair of jeans and three pairs of panties into the backpack, then tossed in the plastic bottle of codeine pills. The muggy heat had finally broken, and there was a chill in the air. I pulled on my leather jacket, which I suddenly realized was going to be an ordeal because of the cast. Luckily I was able to force it into the sleeve, though it proved an extremely snug fit.

"By the way, you said you knew some people in New Orleans."

"Yeah," she reached over to the dresser for a piece of scrap paper and a pen, then sat down on the bed. "A couple of my crazy cousins. They're brothers. Weird thing is they're related to Ennis Lacey, too."

I gave her a strange look.

"Yeah, I know. Miscegenation!" She laughed. "Rumor has it anyway. Supposedly he's their father, but he claims not to be. Ennis went out with my Auntie Jo back in the day…when Jo was turnin' tricks. He was her pimp, got her pregnant, an' she decided to have 'em. They grew up in Macon while Ennis was running coke up from Miami to Atlanta and had his little HQ there for a time. Before he made it big and moved farther west along the gulf. These two boys, ooh, lemme tell you. A handful. Played music in Memphis and Nashville. Got drafted and went to Vietnam. Came back all fucked up. Stoneman and Willie. Stoneman is blind, and Willie's got one wooden leg. Both have *café au lait* complexions. They play music in the square now, down the street from Ennis' house in the quarter. It drives Ennis batshit. Hardly anybody knows their connection. Ennis' older brother, Dix, is in the Klan, you know. Wouldn't do to taint the bloodline. Ennis occasionally gives Stoneman and Willie money to keep their mouths shut. Anyway…you have anything freaky go down, they'll help you out."

"Doesn't sound like they're in too good a shape to help anybody."

"You don't know these two. They can take care of themselves just fine. They wouldn't've made it back from Nam otherwise." She handed me the paper with a phone number. "They're not always there. That's a rooming house. But you call that number and tell whoever that you're a friend of mine, you'll hear from them."

I hugged her.

On the way to the bus stop, Janine filled me in on some things that had happened at the Milk Train.

"Brenda told me that before I got there, Eli was talkin' shit about Ray. Him and Jeannie both were talkin'."

"Jeannie? She was there?"

"Yeah. And she had her hair fixed just like mine and was dressed in a similar outfit. She usually hates for us to be dressed alike."

"Eli and her. What a pair."

"Jeannie left as soon as I got there. But she and Eli sure were chummy. Kind of disgusting. After you left with Sonny to go to the doctor, there was another guy that came in. Some pal of Eli, though Eli was treatin' him like shit. An older guy with a pasty face in a leisure suit. His name's Harry. Mort said he drove in with Eli from El Paso."

We'd pulled up in front of the closed library, which is where the New Orleans-bound bus would stop before continuing on.

"I don't like this, Janey. I don't understand any of it. Lorna told me Ray knocked over some place in El Paso that was mob-connected. That's where Eli comes in. It's the main reason I'm goin' to see Mr. Raindrop...Ennis."

"Fuck."

"Try to talk to Ray, if you can find him."

She nodded. "Don't worry. Just take care of yourself and don't be anxious about things here. I'll hold down the fort."

The bus pulled up. I hugged Janine again and got out.

The Greyhound had been about two-thirds full, and I'd headed right towards the back, a couple rows up from the tiny restroom. I'd gotten two seats to myself on the right side, slinging my backpack on the one next to the window, then settling across it with my now feverish forehead pressed against the chilly glass. It must've been the broken arm and the painkillers. We'd only been out of Mystic for a half an hour on a scary, narrow, two-lane highway when rain started to come down in sheets. I wrapped the long leather jacket tight around me, ignoring the crewcut-headed, hatchet-faced fat man across the aisle who kept glancing at my legs.

I was dozing in-and-out of a codeine reverie.

The first dream I had was about the pasty-faced man in the leisure suit that Janine had told me about. A man I'd never even met. Harry. He seemed to be some kind of cop, a Federal one, and he was infatuated with Eli for both personal and professional reasons. He was a bad cop and a gutless one, an unscrupulous man who manipulated people. There were flashes of what I imagined his face looked like, him stealing into a broken-down back pew of a converted barn-turned-church, a place of worship rented out by one of those snake-handling sects – I think they're loosely affiliated under the banner of the Church of Jesus Christ with Signs Following, or some such. Lester was there with Lucky, and it was the first time Lucky was going to take up serpents. Lucky was sweating bullets. Lester was behind him and, being shorter, had to stand on tiptoe to whisper encouragement in Lucky's ear. The congregation looked to be a bunch of hayseeds –

farm folks and illegal still-owners, snake handlers and strychnine drinkers whose faces were brown from the sun and seemed to be cut out of hard, wrinkled leather. They were singing a deafening, caterwauling hymn that sounded like an Ohio Players song – which made me laugh in my half-sleep. Why did these people want to, need to, handle poisonous snakes? Their souls looked like they were shriveled up inside, sucked dry by the serpents of their bosses in the mines and factories and tiny convenience marts and the ginormous all-purpose stores that sold guns as well as groceries. Didn't they deal with enough human snakes in their everyday lives? Did they have to take every goddamn thing ever written down in scripture literally? Maybe it was the only way they knew how to fight back against the misfortune and tragedy that ran rampant through their blood and dogged them even in their sleep.

Then something happened in the dream – a tiny someone appeared out of the corner of my eye but kept vanishing at the periphery of my vision.

Lucky had a beautiful, sinewy copperhead out now, gently cradling it in his long, lecherous fingers, lifting the reptile to show the congregation he'd made his bones, he'd had the cojones to go all the way, when suddenly little April Pyecroft walked down the aisle, propelled by the guiding hand of corrupt lawman Harry. April – I hadn't thought about her in days; now here she was. Where'd she come from? Did the distant relatives she was staying with in Macon belong to this sect?

I felt as if I was there in one of the back pews, straining and stretching my neck to see. But I couldn't move. More than my arm was broken – my whole body and spirit was crushed. I sat in a crippled mass with Aunt Vivian's arm around my slumped and twisted shoulders. Harry sat across the aisle from me, licking his lips, dividing his time between staring at my pelvis and at April's bottom.

April stopped in front of Lucky. He smiled down at her and handed over the snake to her outstretched hands. There were "oohs" and "awwhhs" from the congregation, but their admiration was cut short as the big-mouthed copperhead snapped out its jaws and clamped its fangs into April's face.

I jumped awake.

There was a deluge outside the window, trying to pound its way in, like the ocean was crashing waves against the side of the bus. I stared around me, groggy, tryng to get my bearings. I was shocked to see April standing there in the aisle, gazing down on me with wide eyes. I reached out to her, and she gave a low cry of alarm as she darted away.

"April!"

A gaggle of bobbing heads popped up, turning to stare at me.

I closed my eyes for a few seconds and, when I opened them again, I realized that the little girl wasn't April at all, just some other misbegotten child being hustled through the night by a barely stitched-together couple a few seats ahead. They had angry expressions on their tight and haggard faces.

I shook my head in disgust, mostly at myself for succumbing to whatever fever dream had possessed me, and I sank back, hunkering down across my pack, my forehead against the sobering chill of the moist glass.

Then I was in another dream.

There was this punk-rock band that had come through Mystic a couple years before, right after Ray was inducted. I'd been bored and had convinced them to let me hitch a ride with them in their van to Athens where they were playing their gig. I'd offered to man their merchandising table, hawking t-shirts and albums and cassettes and CDs. Since then they'd gotten bigger, been on the cover of Rolling Stone. There was a married couple who were the lead singers, and they were good people.

Now they lived in a rundown, but plenty big, sprawling house in Playa del Rey, on the west coast near the Los Angeles airport. That's where they were in this dream anyway, and I was visiting them. It was very sunny, and they had a lot of friends, mostly women, out by the backyard pool with all their kids. Bobby, the lead singer husband, was off somewhere, probably on a beer run, and there was a large punch-bowl on a picnic table out back on the concrete patio. The kids were specifically warned off, told that it was adult stuff. Mina, the wife lead singer, whispered to me that there was some kind of hallucinogen in it. I don't remember what she called it, but it must have been something like MDA, the way everyone was acting. It was strange, all the folks that had partaken sported blue lips stained from the brew. I shied away from indulging, having a sixth sense the syrupy stuff wasn't healthy. Mina and I went in through the open, sliding glass doors. I followed her down a short hall to the bedroom.

The whole place was a white-trash mess from the kids running riot. It was sparsely furnished with second-hand furniture. Mina and I fell down on the unmade mattress, laughing at something or other. Then

I got serious when I noticed her sniffling and licking her blue purple lips in a druggy way. Suddenly I knew for sure there was a toxic chemical in the punch – a mysterious element, some kind of phosphate and a heavy metal, ingredients that the government used in nerve gas. I tried to explain it to Mina, to warn her off taking any more, but she pooh-poohed the idea, saying I was nuts. She was the one who was nuts – the chemical was already affecting her, causing her tattooed arms to twitch in uncontrolled spasms. The toxin was also doing bizarre things to the illustrations on her skin, making the blue-and-black-inked figures dance and distort into mutilated shapes.

Then there was a noise of people laughing on the pool deck, and we stumbled back outside to find Bobby was home. He had a case of beer in one arm, and he was pushing a wheelbarrow with three of their daughters with his free hand. He laughed and unceremoniously dumped them into the pool with a deafening splash that got me wet. A huge, overly-frisky Irish setter was following Bobby, jumping all over him as he turned around and spotted me. He smiled a face-splitting smile and wrapped his arms around me, glad to see that I'd made it into town.

I woke again, drenched in a shivery sweat. I was getting kind of scared that maybe something was really, really wrong with me. It felt sure enough like I had a good-size fever.

There was a roar of thunder that drowned the roaring of the bus, and then a white blaze of lightning blotted out my frightened reflection staring back at me from the smeary, fogged window. The maw of the storm was devouring us.

I fell into an unconscious state again, vaguely tormented by the constant throbbing in my cast-encased forearm. The pulse of the ache beat through my body, much as if my heart was caged there, strangling and twisting in the pulse of my wrist. It informed every image and emotion when I returned to my tortured dreamland.

I was in some nocturnal landscape of urban ghetto blight – Baltimore, I think – trundling along over buckled, weed-choked sidewalks with a gang of denim-jacketed thugs. But I wasn't me – I was Jake Platt, the garage owner from Mystic. I didn't have Jake's usual shaved head, though; I had a conked, teddy-boy pompadour that wouldn't have looked out of place atop the head of Link Wray or Hasil Adkins. I was wearing a charcoal-grey suit coat over a black-silk shirt and black jeans. Somehow I knew I was long dead in the time frame of this nightmare. So was Eli and Jeannie and Lucky and Lester, and so many others. Janine wasn't around. She wasn't dead – I just wasn't sure what had happened to her. Lorna was in the penitentiary, on death row at Metro State Prison up near Atlanta. Ray was still alive, too, but he was hiding out from Mr. Raindrop and his minions.

And I, Jake, had been corralled and threatened into helping those very minions track Ray down. That's when I realized that corrupt lawman Harry was leading our bedraggled posse.

We stopped in front of a fucked-up, abandoned townhouse with a boarded-up door. Harry was staring obsessively at the sidewalk. He motioned to me, hissing my name in a bitchy rasp, then pointing when I'd reached his side. There was a thin trail of blood, a barely visible trickling path of nearly black scarlet that had spattered up the walkway as the unwilling donor leaked out tiny drops of life. They wound their twisted way up five crushed and rotten wood steps, right to the cusp of the threshold of the boarded door.

Harry put a *faux* friendly arm around my shoulder, a gesture that made me tremble, and then whispered words of coaxing betrayal into my ear. He had threatened to kill my crippled mother and my retarded brother if I didn't follow through. Somehow I knew, there were faint odds that they or any of the rest of us would still be breathing in a week's time. But I did as he instructed, gingerly stepping onto the rotting wood at the sides of the steps where it would be the least likely to creak or give way. I pushed open the boarded door, which really wasn't boarded at all. Right away an extremely narrow stairway appeared in front of me. My heart was in my throat, and my arm pounded and thundered with pain as I ascended each carpeted step. I could vaguely make out flickering green candlelight at the top of the stairs. As I neared the top, I saw the walls around the steps were narrowing, closing in so barely the width of my body could make it through. I had to angle sideways to squeeze in. There was no hall up there at the peak; the steps emptied into a microscopic bedroom bathed in lime-green light.

Ray lay there on the bed, atop a mattress on an old-fashioned iron frame, on white sheets that were no longer white because they were smeared with blood. Ray was on his back, shuddering with fever in the fluttering dimness of a votive candle in green glass. His white shirt was open, and I could see the bullet wound in his left side, gurgling with an extremely slow, even trickle. I could just make out that the left sides of his face and body were scarred with burns from an inferno I could vaguely recall happening in Mystic.

"Hello, Jake."

For a few seconds I couldn't answer.

"To what do I owe the pleasure?"

I gulped. "Ennis Raindrop's boys got ahold of me. You know, Harry and some of the other psychos? They got my mama and my brother."

"That's too bad, Jake. We all got our problems. As you can see, things aren't going too swell for me, either."

"Difference is, Ray, I never did anything to get them riled up."

"No, Jake. You just occasionally headed down to Miami at the behest of Mama and Ennis and Lucky to make the occasional pick-up from the Columbians. You only brought in ephedrine from out of state so Lucky's girls could keep their meth lab cooking. You just stripped down cars that seemed to materialize out of thin air from Atlanta and Macon and filed down their VIN numbers and helped Lorna and Lucky sell off what was left. You were a good little smurf, carrying out your tasks with a gleam in your eye and a song in your heart."

He was right. I wasn't any better.

Then I noticed that his left hand lying across his stomach had a WWII military issue .45 revolver clutched in its fist. He raised it slightly till it was pointing at my belly, and then he slowly pulled on the trigger till it made a cracking sound, spitting out a thin tongue of yellow flame that I felt pierce me in the gut.

I sprang awake to see that the dawn was slowly filtering through the trees on the outskirts of Hattiesburg.

Chapter 18

Aunt Vivian is a lovely woman.

Her husband was one of those people that I mentioned earlier who delight in being a prick. His name was Micah Bill Houlihan, although I called him "Formica Bill" due to his cold, hard heart towards me and everyone else. His one saving grace was that he loved Vivian dearly and made her the exception. He treated her differently than anyone else in the world, much different than even his regular blood kin who he went to church with every Sunday. Like Vivian and my mother, he was half-Cherokee on his mother's side, and there was a constant war going on inside him between the Irish and the Indian parts.

He was very late to pick me up from the abandoned gas station that served as Hattiesburg's sole west-side bus stop. I huddled there sitting on my backpack, assailed with hot and cold flashes of fever, trying to stay warm under the rusted old awning spanning the long-unused gas pump islands. I hugged my leather jacket around me as the grey world wept and dripped, trying to decide if it should pour down more water as it suffocated the sun, its light gasping for air from beneath grey-black quilts of clouds that continually passed over it.

Under the plaster cast and a fuzzy blanket of codeine,

my fractured arm throbbed with a dull, nausea-inducing ache.

Finally, he arrived, grumbling that church services with his sisters and ancient mother came first. His 1965 Chevy chugged in uneven stops and starts, and he would not turn his ruddy, grey-stubbled face to acknowledge me, even after I'd ignored his bad temper and bussed him good-naturedly on his cheek as I climbed in the front seat beside him.

"Do my rheumy eyes deceive me? Looks you had yerself a spot o' trouble."

"Looks that way." I offered no further elaboration, and we rode in strained silence till we reached their old, white clapboard house about twenty blocks distant.

Aunt Vivian knew the distinctive sound of her mate's automobile, and she came out onto the sagging porch to greet us, smiling.

That drizzly, confused-weather day in Hattiesburg, she was lovelier than the last time I'd seen her, years past. She'd already become lovelier and more loving still, so, so long ago, while living with me, cleansed from her bitterness by not only the affliction of her blindness – which maybe would have never done it all by itself – but by the added fact she'd entered into a deep compact with me of shared responsibility and affection.

And here she was again, on that last day I might ever see her – lovelier, if that was possible. She was a testament to grace. Not a grace from some supernatural presence, but grace from coming through the fire. Seeing her, feeling her tight, strong embrace all around me, made me buck up and stop feeling sorry for myself. The events of that last week or so had brought so much to the top, nightmarish things that had accumulated days and nights, months and months on end. Events which conspired to hold my head under warm swamp water till I gave up and drowned. Seeing Vivian made me realize I had strength inside of me – I would refuse to let anything or anyone lick me. I would not knuckle under or be beat down.

Formica Bill had adjourned to the den in the back of the house to watch football on the old RCA color television, leaving us two women alone in the front. We walked out onto the porch, Vivian feeling her way with her cane, then stepping down onto an overgrown brick walkway that snaked around the house. We stopped at a long, wooden bench swing hanging between two ash trees, and Vivian handed me the towel she had draped over her shoulder, instructing me to wipe down and dry the residual rain from the peeling, white-painted surface.

I'd debated with myself whether to tell her all that'd been going on with me and had decided to go ahead. I told her pretty much everything, leaving out the drugs part. I told her about Ernie and Fitz, about Eli, about my New Orleans assignment from Lorna and about Ray coming back, refusing to speak to me.

For a couple of minutes, she just sat there, thinking I guess, letting the lukewarm morning breeze fan her face.

"Well, girl, you really have crawled into a prize booby trap. Can't say I didn't think something like this would happen eventually, you stayin' there in Mystic. The town's bad. Always has been. There's always been a lot of outlaws in that town. Sounds like it's only got worse since I was there. You know, it's a coincidence, you bringin' all this up today. Bill's nephew is a state's attorney in Georgia and was just down here last week visitin'. He's investigatin' corruption, drugs, illegal gamblin' in small towns. You should talk to him."

"I can't do that, Vivian."

"Why the hell not? I'll give you his card. I got it somewhere's on top of my bedroom chest of drawers. His name's Steven Marcus Masterson. A good boy. Ambitious, but nice."

"I can't, Vivian. I do something like that, Ray'd get caught up in the net along with Lorna and the rest. And my life wouldn't be worth a damn. I'd be killed, sure."

She sighed. "Suit yerself. I can't imagine why you told me all this, if you weren't lookin' for my counsel."

"It's not I don't value your advice. I just needed to tell the story to someone outside of Mystic. In case anything happens to me down the line."

"I can tell you got a bad feelin'."

"I do."

"Well, then..."

"I feel like I'm on a runaway train and can't get off. If it wasn't for Ray, maybe I'd see my path clear to get out."

"It's certain he's turned against you."

"I don't know that. I can't believe it. I've really hurt him somehow. I can't help but think there's some kind of misunderstanding I don't know about. And if I could tidy that up, maybe – "

"Maybe...a lot of maybes."

"Vivian, you know I'm still in love with him. I can't just give up."

She nodded. "I guess. It's hard for me to understand. He's not

as bad as the rest, but I've never understood what you see in him. He's
a good-for-nothing. All the same, I wish you luck. You're mixed up
with a nest of vipers, honey. I wish you would talk to Bill's nephew. It
might make a difference."

"I can't. Not now. Who knows how I'll feel in a few months."

"If yer still amongst the livin'." She grimaced, frustrated after
she said those last words, then got up by herself, walking towards the
brick walk and the house, tapping with her cane, leaving me sitting on
the creaking swing.

We had a nice, cozy dinner that night, Bill biting his tongue and being
sweet, cooking and serving us fried chicken, collard greens, black-eyed
peas and homemade lemonade.

After we were done eating, I turned in. I had to be up early the
next morning to catch the bus to New Orleans.

Bill drove me over there about 8:00 AM. Right before I got out of the
car, he returned to his old, nasty self.

"Connie, I don't want you to see Vivian again."

"She tell you to say that?"

"No. I'm tellin' you. Yer a no-good lil' tramp and, from what I
gather, always have been. You really upset Vivian yesterday with that
talk. I don't know what you told her, and I don't care. I just want you to
stay out of our lives. Her life. She doesn't need the aggravation."

"Listen, you self-righteous son-of-a-bitch, I'll see her anytime I
want unless she tells me different, unless she tells me herself. She's my
only living blood kin. I love her. She feels the same about me. She told
me so this mornin' before I left."

I grabbed my pack and slammed the door in his turning-red
face. He roared off just as the bus pulled to the curb.

The bus trip to New Orleans was a lot different than the one I took to
Hattiesburg. The New Orleans leg of my trip, my ordeal, I couldn't
sleep at all. I was already halfway through my codeine, and it was
creating a tight inner screen of barb wire around the inside of my brain.
Oh, God, what was I doing? The sun was playing its hide-and-seek
games behind dirty, toxic clouds dripping corrosive poison drops from
big money industries that were tucked away in backwater swamps of
rural poverty. Everywhere in that lush green, sticky wet countryside
there was the odor of death, of sulphur and corruption, open sores in
the earth appearing out of nowhere with blossoms of burning venom

destroying the wild, the feral and the pure. The oil and the chemical combines were paying off politicians who were no better, no different than Mr. Raindrop and Lorna Diamond. By all visible evidence, they were worse, with the sociopathic, coiled serpent, subhuman mindset of an Eli. I remembered Janine and me joking about the polluted water we bathed in and we were all drinking in Mystic. And when I tried to close my eyes and blot out my negative thoughts, I recalled one afternoon walking along the creek in the woods outside of town – a plume of scarlet phosphorous dumped by some biker crank chemist swirling downstream rust-red through the previously crystal-clear water.

Before I knew it, we were in the heart of New Orleans. I got off in the middle of the French Quarter. I'd lost track of all time. I didn't have a watch and couldn't tell from the sky of it was early or late afternoon. Black clouds were drifting low, blocking out the sun. I needed to find a phone. Lorna had told me to call her once I got in, and she would give me direction to Ennis "Raindrop" Lacey's palace of sin.

I had trouble finding a payphone that worked, then when I did, calling collect, Lorna's boy Friday had to go scour the house to find her. There were all kinds of people parting like a drunken sea around where I stood, the phone sticking up on an island in an ocean of human flotsam: square tourists, hep musician types, bikers, elderly ladies with their plastic bags, drug-addled homeless…even a trio of nuns.

Lorna came on the line, cold and efficient, asking what was the closest intersection. I told her, and she rattled off concise directions and the address to Mr. Raindrop's. I'd already bought a pint of bourbon and, when I bid her fond farewell and hung up, I immediately scrawled them on the back of the liquor's paper bag.

I stood there paralyzed for a moment. I felt terribly alone. Formica Bill's hateful words came back to me, echoing in my skull. I wondered if Aunt Vivian really was the lovely woman I thought she was. When I left Hattiesburg, was her telling me she loved me just bullshit? Was she having her poisonous husband do the dirty work in some kind of passive aggresive swich-and-bait routine? I couldn't see it. Not her. She would have had a fit if she'd heard what he told me.

My paranoia was getting the better of me.

Something stung my heart, and I realized I was dwelling on Ray again and how he had given me that spiteful stare as he'd peeled out of the Milk Train lot. I had to shake off that black cloud.

Turning, I saw a small park square laid out before me.

It was just strange enough to be true. Was the world really that small? Unless I missed my guess, there were Janine's cousins – and Ennis' bastard sons – Stoneman and Willie, playing steel drums and guitar from where they were perched on a low brick wall.

They kept playing when I stopped in front of them, singing comments and questions at me as if it was part of their shtick.

"White girl all alone in the Big Easy, makin' friends and impressin' sad men nearin' the bitter end, on the brink of disaster, fallin' faster an' faster. What this woman got beneath her dress that could make a grown man cry? Fallin' and moanin' in the late afternoon, makin' her rivals swoon and change their tune…"

"I'm…"

"…Connie Eustace McQueen livin' in a world cold and mean, lucky to have a sista friend name Janine…"

I wasn't sure which was Stoneman and which was Willie, but the one with the guitar – the blind one – put down his instrument. "Janine called us, honeychile."

"You headin' into the pit." The one-armed man stopped playing his steel drums. "You best keep yer wits about you all da time, girl. Dem folks down the block like to call the shots, all down the line."

Janine hadn't told me, but they were identical twins, just like her and Jeannie. They were both dressed in floppy, furry white pimp hats, brocaded white jumpsuits with rhinestones and sequins lined along the seams.

"Which one of you's Willie, which one's Stoneman?"

The blind one, who had only one other difference in his very light chocolate face – a gap-toothed grin – leaned his guitar against the brick wall and raised his hands. "I'm Willie."

He reached out, and I clasped his extended palm.

Stoneman leaned over, reaching out his lone left hand. I shook it, too.

"That leaves only one o' us that could be Stoneman. How you doin,' girl? Looks like you had a little aggravation." He pointed at the cast.

I just nodded.

"Keep an eye out for the ole man down the street. Mr. Raindrop ain't the kind to fall on you in a gentle shower. No, no, he fall more like stingin' stones in a hailstorm."

"He is a liar and a cheat, a man who lies for the pure pleasure it gives him."

"I can take care of myself. Sometimes."

"Hopefully this be one o' dem times. I think so, yeah."

"We'll see." I was starting to talk like them, using heavy symbols. "I've consigned myself to the whirlwind."

"We aware, girl. We here for you, you need us."

Chapter 19

I stopped at an ancient but beautifully preserved mahogany door, stained with a varnish more black than brown, with the vague, subliminal hint of the color of blood. There was a gnarled brass knocker of a woman's head and breasts at about eye level, which I put to use.

No point in trying to make out like I was feeling courageous. I was scared, right down to my toenails.

The door slowly opened, and two women in their early twenties appeared, one dark-complected, a white brunette with thick, sensual lips who was dressed like Marie Antoinette and the other, a pale Asian with cartoonishly big almond eyes and a rosebud-shaped mouth, clad the same.

"Lorna Diamond sent me with a package for Mr. Raindrop." I felt a fool playing Ennis' game, using that alias.

They made a space between them to let me pass, and I walked into a very dark, high-ceilinged foyer. The white girl floated past me, indicating with a backward glance that I was to follow. An imposing, curved staircase lurked in the shadows to my left.

The house was gigantic. From the street, you'd never have guessed it was so big.

Suddenly we took a turn to the right, into a sparsely furnished sitting room with hardwood floors. There were four other girls of various shapes, sizes and ethnicities clad in mostly antique French lingerie, lounging about on settees, low velvet sofas and deep plush easy chairs. The upholstery and drapery in the room was color-coordinated, alternating between a dark fir green and a queasy-looking purple. The curtains on the far wall were pulled to reveal tall windows that stretched almost to the ceiling. A tangled tropical garden lay outside in an enclosed courtyard, grey and sickly in the anemic sunlight that was trying to fight its way through the storm clouds. It was hot in the room. A roaring blaze crackled in the five foot tall fireplace.

Then I noticed him. It couldn't have been anyone else. He was clad in black dress slacks, a white frilly shirt open to his navel, revealing his sunken 60-year-old, grey-haired chest. An undone bow tie hung limply, the ends dangling on either side of his collar. Seated on the floor beneath the window, he had his pants rolled up above his knees, with the bare bottom half of his shriveled legs disappearing into an open floor vent of the house's antiquated central heating system.

His eyes sparkled as I approached him, and he smoothed back his rumpled, thinning red hair and straightened his wispy moustache. His voice had a quality of insincere buoyancy.

"Connie Eustace McQueen, if I don't miss my guess. Right on time, too. I do delight in people who are punctual, who keep their appointments. It looks, though, that you are a bit worse for wear." He nodded at my arm.

"I'm okay. I'm a little parched. I need to take a pill anyway, if you have some water." The Asian girl from the front door wafted soundlessly to my side, handing me a glass practically before I could finish the sentence. I sipped it, then took out the pill bottle and shook one into my palm, then tossed it into my mouth.

Damn, it was hot. Sweat was running down my forehead and behind my ears.

"Forgive the heat, my dear. I have famously poor circulation. I'm sorry if you're finding it a bit stuffy."

I timidly glanced about. "It's all right. I can live with it."

"That's the spirit." He picked up a brandy snifter from his side and indulged himself with a meager taste. He smiled broadly as he set it down again. "I understand you have a package for me from Mrs. Diamond?"

I sat down on the arm of a couch, cradling my backpack in my cast-covered arm and dug deep, rummaging through the clothes.

I pulled out the wrapped cash, then leaned over and tucked it squarely into his upraised palm.

"Delightful. Lorna is so responsible." His freakishly-wide smile made it seem as if his face was going to split in two. "Bernice will show you to your room, Connie. Please don't be shy about letting her know if you need anything. A bath, dinner – anything."

I followed Marie Antoinette out and towards the staircase.

The next thing I remember was waking up naked, shackled by one wrist to a single wrought-iron bedstead, lying atop a thin, lumpy mattress. There was another girl, with dishwater-blonde hair, also naked, handcuffed to the bed next to me. I found out later that the high-ceilinged room we were locked in was on the top third floor of Raindrop's house. Or should I say his dope slave brothel? I was high as fuck, and I realized immediately what they were doing from the numerous black-and-blue tracks in the crook of my upraised, chained right arm.

I'd thought at first the girl was asleep, since her eyes were closed. But she wasn't. She just seemed that way because she was so heavy-lidded from the heroin.

"Finally awake, hunh?" she drawled.

I tried to sit up but couldn't.

"My name's Sadie. What's yours?"

I was angry, and I wanted to tell her to go fuck herself, but my mouth felt as if it was stuffed with cotton.

"You thirsty? This stuff really gives you cottonmouth. Plus you bein' out for two days straight."

I turned over on my side. There was a doggy dish between the beds full of water.

"You want a drink, that's what you have to use. They make us kneel down and lap it up."

Despite the high, I was too physically miserable to feel humiliated and rolled off the bed onto the dusty floor, trying to awkwardly position my cast so I wasn't leaning on it. I lapped greedily at the water.

"Don't drink too much right off. You'll just puke it up." She giggled moronically. "There's a bedpan under your bed, you need to perform any bodily function. I got one, too. Frick and Frack will empty them when they come in to give us our shots."

I sat back on my haunches, kneeling, staring dumbly at my cellmate.

"You got cute tits. Bigger than mine. I got lil' boy tits." She was pretty far gone.

"How long have you been here?"

She didn't seem to understand my question. Was she brain-damaged to boot?

"You still haven't told me your name," she repeated petulantly, "I told you mine."

"Connie. How long you been chained in here, Sadie."

"Longer than you, lemme tell you. You're here long enough, you start losin' track of what day it is, how long you been layin' here. One thing I learned, you gotta keep from layin' too long in one position, or you'll start to get bedsores."

"Something to look forward to."

"No, it ain't."

Jesus!

"You know what I look forward to, Connie?"

I didn't answer.

"Come on, what do you think I look forward to?"

I rolled my eyes. "I don't know...when they finally unchain you?"

She snorted with laughter. "No, silly! The shots. Plus Frick and Frack will fuck you if you want. Sometimes even if you don't want."

"Sounds lovely."

"It is." She wasn't being funny – she was serious.

I was trying to focus my thoughts on how I could escape, but the dope kept dragging me down. I was pretty scared, but I'd hit an emotional ceiling. I was so high, the fear had no edge on it.

"Where have they got our clothes?"

She wagged her head towards a scuffed-up door on the other side of her bed near the window. "Closet. Don't worry."

"You don't mind lying here naked as a jaybird?"

She shook her head, changing the subject. "I have to admit, I am looking forward to workin' for Mr. Raindrop."

"You are?"

"Hell, yeah! I know better now."

"What do you mean, now?"

"When he first invited me to dinner, I didn't know that's what he wanted. When I found out, you know, when he told me, I got mighty uppity. Told him to go fuck himself. Next thing I knew, here I am, flat on my back, *au naturel*, as the French say. I'd never been high before. Hardest thing I ever touched was whiskey and my boyfriend's dick.

Now I know how awesome it is. I feel so good, long as I keep feelin'
this way, long as they keep pumpin' that sweet nectar into me, I just
don't give a good goddamn."

I had to get away before they could get me strung out like that.
Truth be told, I thought no matter what happened, no matter how much
they got their hooks into me, I could never get to the place where Sadie
was. But I didn't want to take a chance on being wrong.

There was a clank of a key in the lock which made me spring
back on the bed in a prone position, and I defensively crossed my legs.

The guy that came in was what city folks up in the northeastern
part of the country probably call a goombah. He had oily black hair that
smelled of pomade. His white, long-sleeve shirt was half unbuttoned to
reveal a forest of bearish, iron curls on his chest, the sight of which
made me physically ill. His face was covered in five o'clock shadow,
and it sloped into a wolfish grin. He had what looked like a .38 snub-
nose revolver in a shoulder holster. The tray he was carrying he set on
the end of my bed, then sat down beside me.

"Ahh, I see our new visitor finally decided to wake up."

"You got me my shot, Frick?"

Frick ignored her.

"How you feelin'? Your name's Connie, am I right?"

I pulled myself into a sitting position, edging back away from
him.

"Oh, aren't you cute? Still a little shy, are we? That'll change
after a while." He looked at the strung-out, practically panting-with-
anticipation blonde. "Won't it, Sadie?"

She nodded. "Frick, don't be cruel. I need my shot."

Frick smiled and turned his stare at me. "See what I mean? Just
so you know, you get fed once a day at lunchtime. You have to wait till
tomorrow 'cause you were out of it earlier. You understand? Food is
once a day. That's it. But you probably won't be too hungry after some
time passes." He lifted up an already-filled, ready-to-go syringe from
the tray. "Not for food, anyway."

I recoiled.

"Now come on, Connie, don't be stupid. I don't want to have to
get too rough with you. Mr. Raindrop wouldn't like it."

I stretched out my arm, as much as the chain would let me,
giving in. He took a swab of cotton moistened with alcohol, rubbed it
where the other tracks were, tied a piece of thin rubber hose around my
upper muscle, then, using his expert eye, plunged the needle home in
the crook of my elbow. He did it quickly, immediately registering the

vein, sucking up a few drops of blood, then injecting the clear, pure poison. After only a couple of seconds, it felt like someone hit me with a velvet baseball bat. His voice echoed from the top of a dark well as I descended into murky, womblike depths.

"You get three a day, sugar. One at 8 AM, one at 4 PM and one at midnight. But you'll lose track of the time before you know it…"

I nodded in and out of consciousness while he gave Sadie her dose, then stripped and climbed onto the mattress with her. She laughed stupidly, overcome with her own depravity, and raised her arms to welcome him as he penetrated between her legs.

I hoped that I would be conscious when they returned with my shot at midnight. I had to get out of that fucking place, and the cover of night would be the best time to do it.

Before either Frick or Sadie came, I nodded off again.

When I awoke, it was dark in the room with barely visible outlines of faint street light coming from the sides of the heavily curtained windows. My eyes gradually grew used to the dimness, and I could spot Sadie, passed out on her side, facing me. Her mouth hung slightly open, and she was snoring. I couldn't be sure till I checked, but I sensed our room was on the rear side of the house.

It was hard to keep track of the passing time. I knew the hour must be drawing near because I was starting to feel a chill and a craving. I hoped whomever came at midnight to administer my dope would be by themselves, because I had a vivid, full-blown fantasy of just exactly what I was going to do. I don't know how long it was that I lay there. It seemed like hours, but that could have been my ever-growing apprehension of maybe getting myself killed.

At last, the noise of the key came in the lock, and the door swung slowly open to reveal a silhouetted figure.

A faint echo of Dixieland jazz filtered up from the ground floor.

He stood there, his features obscured as he studied us, and I squinted at the comparative brightness, the glare shooting over his shoulders into my pinned pupils. He switched on the light and closed the door with one hand, holding the tray with the two syringes in the other. I closed my eyes for a couple of seconds. The light hurt.

I deduced this man must be who Sadie called Frack, because it sure wasn't Frick from earlier. He was dressed much the same, except he had on a paisley shirt. A .38 snub nose was also tucked into a leather sling holster under his left shoulder. This man did not have the primitive animal magnetism of Frick. He was only about 5'6", skinny as hell, with a noticeable limp in his shorter left leg. I felt encouraged. He looked easier to tackle than Frick, the Italian lothario who'd banged the hell out of Sadie. But there was still a frightening aspect to him. He had a narrow, corpse-like face, a scar down his right cheek, a slim cigar protruding from his teeth and a receding hairline. Being the quiet type, he didn't say a word as he sat down at the foot of Sadie's mattress first and prepared her shot. That's when I noticed she was already sitting up, cross-legged before him, eagerly anticipating her approaching nocturnal reverie.

"Hey, Bilbo. How goes it?"

He was unresponsive and businesslike, totally stoic. He took her arm and patiently scanned it for a viable vein that hadn't already collapsed. Finding a likely prospect, he rapidly accomplished the procedure, and Sadie's half-closed eyes rolled up into her head for a split second before she dropped like a stone back onto her pillow.

I sat up, swinging my legs over the side of the mattress

I had to gauge my blow just so, at just the right moment, or I'd be done for. He was sitting there to my left, the dope-filled rig in his right hand. When he reached out across my lap to take hold of my right wrist, I smashed upwards into his mouth with my cast-covered left forearm. He gave a surprised "oomph" of hurt as he went down on the floor. For a second, a current of live wire pain tingled through my cracked, up-till-then healing bone and nearly blinded me.

When I looked, I saw that he was still conscious and grabbing for his gun. I had to yank at my fortunately long shackles to pull the scrawny bedframe with me. I leapt onto him, straddling his lap and bringing the cast down again hard across his face. His arms, his whole body, went limp. As I clutched at my battered cast with my good hand, drawing it up through a cloud of red hot, branding-iron torture, I noticed his eyes were still open and glazed. There was a purple contusion on his left temple, and I abruptly realized I'd killed him. A horrible thought occurred to me. What if he didn't have the key to the handcuffs on him? If he didn't, I was good and truly fucked.

I pulled him along the floor to give myself more slack in the shackles then, panicking, rummaged through his pants and shirt pockets, only to come up empty-handed. I turned him over and miraculously there they were, hanging from a clip on a belt loop of his trousers. I frantically tore at them, ripping his pants. There were four keys on the ring – a car key, the room key and two small keys which had to be for our chains. I unlocked my cuffs and shakily stood up.

I nearly fainted, despite the adrenaline coursing through me. Then I saw something else, an oblong of shiny black plastic that had fallen out of Bilbo's or Frack's or whatever his name was' back pocket. It was a small walkie-talkie. On cue, it crackled to life with static and a tinny voice, "Hey, Hudson, got the caterers leavin' now through the back lot." Another voice responded. "That's a roger, Sammy boy."

My arm was killing me. I looked longingly at the remaining full syringe on the tray, then mentally kicked myself. As I rolled the dead thug over to pull out his gun, I raised my eyes to check Sadie's consciousness status. Still out. I took a step up onto her bed, then came down in front of the closet on the other side. I wouldn't get too far leaving naked with just the .38!

Not all of my clothes were in the dank, foul-smelling little chamber. My jeans, sweater and backpack were gone, but my long black leather jacket, my skirt and halter top hung from a sturdy wooden hanger.

I tucked the gun into one of the jacket pockets, then felt around for the secret pocket in the rear near the bottom hem. It felt like the expense money Lorna gave me was still there. I opened it and sighed with relief as I felt the crisp leaves of folded cash. I quickly put on the skirt, the top and, once more with awkward difficulty, slipped on the jacket. The cast was starting to shred, to slowly come apart from the rugged abuse, and it kept getting caught in the left sleeve seams. At last, I managed it, and felt almost whole again. Then I realized there were no shoes in the closet, and that I'd have to hightail it barefoot. I looked in the full-length mirror that was hooked to the inside of the closet door. I was a fucking mess.

Sadie was too out of it, so I decided against trying to rescue her. Besides, bringing the strung-out head case along would undoubtedly destroy any chance I had of escape.

There was no one in the dimly lit third-floor corridor as I edged out of the dope dungeon. After relocking the door, I stood there for a few seconds trying to assess the best of two decidedly less than desirable routes. The main staircase lay to my left, giving off light from below. The Dixieland music had ceased, replaced by a low murmur of drunken, laughing voices. Luckily, to my right, I spotted another smaller staircase, no doubt originally built for servants. I started down those uncovered hardwood steps and realized it was just as well I had no shoes. My tread was barely audible, though the wood occasionally gave off complaining creaks as it felt my weight. The passage downstairs was virtually dark, and I had to carefully watch my footing to make sure I didn't go hurtling headlong to a broken neck.

I had to keep an eye out for Raindrop's minions or any of those girls I'd met downstairs as I passed the second floor. The corridor was much better lit, though still dim, full of decadent green and purple lamps lining the walls. Along with the dark stained wood, it seemed to be Raindrop's color motif for the whole brothel. There was a drunken old man with two whores, one black and one Asian, in 18th-century dress, clinging to his arms as they stumbled towards the main staircase.

When I reached the first floor, there was a clamor of pots and pans and the whoosh of hot water in a huge sink. It came from off to the right, from what was probably the kitchen. I passed the bright, open entrance to the scullery and spotted a couple of cooks in white outfits and a trio of tux-clad waiters scurrying back and forth, cleaning up. Directly in front of me was a huge ornate door that I fervently hoped was the house's rear exit. I cracked it open and saw a wooden loading dock with four or five steps descending to a gravel lot filled with five cars and a van. I nervously studied the car key I'd swiped, trying to guess which vehicle it fit. One of the cars was a Mercedes and two others were late-model town cars. Not those. The remaining two were sixties muscle cars: a '65 or '66 Mustang and what I thought might be a '70 Malibu. I was lucky. The key looked like the key to a Chevy or Chrysler, so I figured the only choice was the Malibu. As I crept along the dock towards it, I passed the van and, as I did, the rear driveway to the lot came into view. A husky man stood there in shirt-sleeves, his back to me, smoking a cigarette. I moved quickly to the car, scraping my feet on the wet gravel, slipped in the key, turned it, swung open the door and sank into the leather seat. It was an automatic, thank God! I was having an incredible run of luck. I turned on the ignition, then the lights. The guy in the driveway casually looked behind him, flicked his half-spent smoke out into the darkness and then strolled towards me. I let the car roll slowly forwards, stopping as he came abreast.

"Hi, missy. What're you doin' in Billy's short?"

"There's no more absinthe in the wine cellar. The cook wanted me to go down the street a few blocks. There's a backdoor place that sells it after hours. Billy said to take his car."

"That right? He didn't call me on the radio."

"Well, how else could I have gotten his keys?" I laughed. "I didn't hotwire this baby." My nerves were shredding. When would Billy be missed? When would they find him, white-faced and croaked in the dope dungeon?

He smiled, looking in at the ignition.

"Guess not." He took a step back. "Hey, you don't look too familiar. I don't remember seein' you earlier. You come in through here?"

I shook my head and thought I would take a chance and mention another name I'd heard on dead Billy's radio. I was pretty sure this guy questioning me was named Hudson. "No. Sammy told me to come through the front. Mr. Raindrop wanted to meet me."

He nodded vacantly, lost in trying to figure out if he should get on my case. He produced his walkie-talkie out of nowhere, clicking on the talk button as he raised it to his whiskered lips. "Billy, come in."

"You might not get him. His radio battery went dead, and he was looking around for some fresh ones."

He nodded, doubt clouding his blunt features. "Hey, Sammy, how about you? You there?"

The tinny voice crackled in response. "Yeah? Hud?"

"Roger."

"What the hell you want? I'm busy."

"You send any girls around by the front earlier? To meet the boss?

"You kiddin'? A whole raft of 'em came in that way. Look, chum, I got my hands full. There's a drunk jig musician we got to throw out. Lemme call you back in a sec."

"Roger that, Sammy boy."

I smiled up at him. "So everything okay?"

"Yeah, I guess. Go ahead. I know Billy, and the only way you could have gotten those keys off of him is if he gave 'em to ya."

I forced myself to make my grin wider, then playfully blew him a kiss as I rolled lackadaisically out of the lot.

I wasn't sure in which direction to blow town, and I thought of calling Stoneman and Willie to get directions. But then I reckoned stopping to find a pay phone, when any minute Raindrop's men might be racing after me, was not a prudent idea.

After a long few minutes, I found an on-ramp to the freeway east, then there I was, rocketing towards home. Before I knew it, I'd crossed the Mississippi state line.

My weakness, my hunger, the deep pangs and jitters that were rising up as I came off the dope, made me angry. The anger kept me on overdrive. I was damn lucky I'd only been on the stuff for two or three days, four or five if you counted Janine's dose in Mystic and the codeine pills from Doc Clayburn.

As it was, by the time I dropped down to the highway that went through Enterprise and Dothan, I ended up having to stop every half hour or so to retch pathetically on the side of the road. No amount of dope sickness could quell my rage, and I kept on, my vengeful retribution lying ahead of me in Mystic, my thumping black heart homing in on it like a beacon.

Raindrop's men would be after me. Or maybe he'd just have his partners in Mystic, Van Heusen, Eli – and maybe even Lorna – do his dirty work for him. They'd be only too glad to oblige. I really didn't give a damn anymore. The next time I got boxed into a tight spot, I'd be more alert.

I was certain worse was coming.

I might even end up getting myself snuffed.

But I was going to take as many of those bastards with me as I could.

PART THREE
Ray Diamond
August 1987

Chapter 20

I thought once I got back to Mystic things would work themselves out, and I could take a breather. I needed one. But that wasn't the case. Things were more fucked up than they were before. And the situation kept getting worse.

When I rolled into town after a good four months of horror, I found Eli there – working for Mama. She filled me in on who Eli was and who Red had been. Whose money I'd taken. Mama said it didn't matter if Eli had been the one to waste his dad or not. All Mr. Raindrop and his partners in the west cared about was the money. Then they leveraged a rip-off deal from Mama, a deal she'd supposedly agreed to so the contract out on me would be cancelled.

I haven't talked to Connie. I'd meant to, wanting to find out what that goddamn pornographic photo of her giving head was all about. But I just couldn't, not after I saw her playing with herself up onstage at The Milk Train. What the fuck? Did she just turn into a full-blown whore while I was gone?

I felt like I was a candidate for the lunatic asylum – if I didn't blow my head off first. Every moment I was offered a new snapshot

from hell, and it made me continually question my sanity. What I'd
been through on my odyssey home had been bad enough, but to finally
arrive and be confronted with the whirlpool of deceit and depravity
Mystic was becoming, it made the ground crumble beneath my feet.

When I'd fallen off the train thirty miles or so east of Juarez, I was
deathly ill. I immediately vomited and then, when there was nothing
left to bring up, I retched and dry-heaved until I passed out in the hot
sun. It was some kind of miracle I didn't die out there from the
exposure and dehydration.

I awoke once the night had fallen, and I immediately realized I
wasn't too far from a road. I crawled towards it, but lost consciousness
again just as I reached the warm asphalt. When I came to I don't know
how many hours later, I was in the tumble-down tin and wood shack
of Simon, an old man who could barely speak. Not that he didn't know
Spanish and some English, but he seemed to have been the victim of a
stroke at some point. When he talked, it was slow and with an effort.

Unfortunately, though he was the one who saved me from the
side of the road, when he gave me food and drink, it was contaminated
with the local version of Montezuma's revenge, and I came down with
dysentery. I felt like I was spewing the life right out of me – blood,
water, shit, viscera, everything. I'd be lying there in the shack, sometimes passed out, sometimes half awake in a dream delirium. The slats
in the walls of the shack were exactly like the ribs of a skeleton and,
during the heat of the day, the sun would seep through those cracks,
looking like fire and feeling like radiation, burning everything away
until I was in a white world of conflagration that ate away skin, leaving
nothing but a blistering, blackened shell.

It got bad enough after a couple of weeks that he went for a
doctor. I don't know where he got the money to finally pay him. I don't
think it was any of mine; I don't remember. Miraculously, the old man
didn't find the gun and the cash bag stuffed down my pants till the
doctor arrived and, when he saw what was in the bag, I guess – from
what I learned later – it nearly gave him another stroke. He kept it from
the doctor, and when I had finally regained consciousness and my fever
had gone down, he showed the bag and gun to me, letting me know he
was an honest man. Unbelievable, but true.

Then it was almost a month and a half later. I'd lost a lot of weight and
a lot of brain cells. I needed to move on, and I quizzed the old man
on how I could get a lift further east. It took a while, but he at last got

my drift and explained that his younger brother-in-law, Wendel, would be by there in a few days and could probably give me a ride as far as Matamoros.

It would have to do.

When Wendel came by, Simon began acting strange, like there was something not quite right. Wendel was picking up artifacts the old man had unearthed at a nearby Indian burial site and, while Wendel was loading them into his pick-up, Simon gave me a small leather bag for my money and my gun as well as some cryptic words of advice.

"Arrive to Matamoros. No stay night. No eat there. Go Brownsville across border."

I stared at him, dense and not quite getting it.

He frowned, frustrated. "Matamoros no good." He wagged his finger. "Gringo, no good. Bad for gringo. Remember. No stay night."

I nodded, a little troubled but confident I could deal with whatever he was going on about. I tried to give him some money, but he wouldn't take it. When his back was turned, I stuffed a couple of hundred dollars under the sweat-stained pillow on the cot.

Soon we'd left Simon far behind, and I had to adjust to Wendel's weird personality. He was one big question mark, from the tips of his scuffed-up Beatle boots to the army fatigue dungarees and garish purple polyester shirt he wore, to his googly pop eyes, pencil moustache and the ugly spit curls plastered across his mostly bald, sweaty head.

"You like disco?"

"No."

"You like party? Rock 'n' roll?"

"Yeah."

"Punk rock? Heavy metal?"

"Sometimes."

He laughed.

"How's about whiskey? You like whiskey?"

"Who doesn't?"

He thought that was hilarious.

"Tequila? Mescal?"

I nodded.

That really sent him into a galoomphing fit of amusement, so much so he started coughing, and I thought for a minute we were going to career off the pitch-black road.

"You like girls?

I was getting sick of his questions and gave him a dirty look. It didn't faze him.

"Boys?"

I stared out the windshield into the night. This, he also found a knee-slapping reaction, coughing and spitting as he roared with laughter.

I was on edge. Something was spooking me. I wasn't afraid of Wendel, but there was something about the whole scene that struck me as wrong, and I couldn't put my finger on it.

"You thirsty, there is whiskey under seat."

He had a strange accent.

"My mother is Russian. You wonder my accent, right? Yes, is so. Father Mexican, mother Russian. She came to this country before war, 1930s. Was servant for Trostsky. You heard of? I have relatives all over. Father's brothers – my uncles – are from Puerto Rico. My cousins, too. I have big family. We do many interesting things to make living in this country. What you do?"

I eased up. "Right now, I do nothing."

He laughed. "Nothing! Is good job if you can get!" He slapped my knee as if it was a priceless punchline. "What's matter? Why not drinking? Good for you!"

I reached under the seat and pulled out a half full fifth of Jack Daniels.

"Drink, drink, amigo, my American friend. Jack is good, is it not?"

"Jack is good."

I wasn't sure if I should drink or not. I hadn't had any alcohol since the mescal in Juarez. My stomach was queasy. Of all things, the leg that Munson had run over in Coronado was acting up, throbbing like all get-out. It hadn't bothered me in El Paso or Juarez, and my limp was almost gone. But then in the cab of Wendel's truck, the pain whooshed back. I thought maybe the drink would do me good. I had the jitters, being sick for so fucking long and, on top of it all, carrying that money.

I twisted off the cap and offered it to him first. He gratefully nodded and tossed back a good couple of shots worth, then returned it to me. I drank about the same amount. It burned going down, but it felt good. Maybe that's what I'd needed. A good stiff drink to put me right.

I knew it was going to be a long haul. It was over 800 miles, and Wendel wasn't driving particularly fast. The highway we were on was not in great shape, and he really couldn't go over 60 at any time and not risk going off the shoulder. We were looking at 16 hours at the very least. With stops for gas and food, probably more like 18.

There was a battered plastic baby Jesus attached by a magnet to the dash. Sun-bleached paint peeled off his crown, face and cloak. There was another even more fucked-up plastic icon of an old bearded man with a crutch sitting next to the sacred infant.

Wendel saw me looking at them. He touched the head of Jesus. "Nzambi."

I looked at him, not understanding.

"Nzambi. God of universe. Creator."

I shrugged.

He touched the head of the old man icon.

"Kobayende. Tata Fumbe…King of Dead."

He saw I still didn't quite get it, though I knew it had to be related to some kind of Caribbean religion.

"You hear of Palo?"

"Palo?"

"Palo Mayombe, my friend." He handed the Jack to me and nodded. "Drink, drink, my friend. Good for you." He laughed.

I upended the bottle and took another mouthful. It felt good.

Palo Mayombe. There was a kid from Puerto Rico in my outfit in Coronado. Juan. He'd talked similar shit when he was three sheets to the wind. Mumbling barely intelligible curses at Munson when he was giving us a hard time. Thinking about Munson brought it all back, his goddamn Hemi crushing my leg, and the pain came loping and leaping to pounce on me. My leg throbbed, and I drank another gulp of the sour mash.

I watched the night road unfolding in the beam of the headlights, little winged insects unwittingly sacrificing themselves in accidental kamikaze dives into the windshield. Wendel was something else, talking trash as if he knew exactly what was going through my mind.

"Tiny creatures, no souls. Hundreds die, thousands every night. It goes on for countless centuries. They die…meaningless deaths. Just like man." He paused in mock seriousness, then abruptly laughed a maniacal laugh, trying to elbow me. I refused to look over at him.

There was something going on with that whiskey. I started to think he'd dosed it with a drug. The bugs were exploding right, left and center, but their bodies burst in microscopic pinwheels of yellow light that went purple as the illumination decayed. Beautiful but scary jewels of color cracking apart on the glass.

But he was drinking the bourbon, too. Then again, he was crazy. The ache in my leg suddenly got worse, like flame shooting through my arteries, and there was a flood of bright orange and yellow fire that appeared, flooding the desert plains on both sides of the road, a carpet of combustion imprinting horribly intense patterns of brightness on my irises. I pressed my palms to my sockets, shutting my eyelids as tightly as I could. It did no good. Those fields of fire were still there, slithering and undulating in psychedelic rushes of yellow and red.

Wendel began a low, barely audible laugh, a mirthless sound that gradually grew louder and more manic until he was beating time on the steering wheel to his coughing fits of hysterical amusement.

"Jack is so, so, so good. Am I not correct? He open gates of sanity with few drops, eh?" His laughter echoed in the truck cab, and I suddenly felt like I was going to puke. I cranked the window down just in time, spewing glowing trails of liquid out into the fiery night. When I turned back, Wendel was tossing down several pills with the last of the spiked Jack.

He glanced over. "You want? No sleep. Whoa, yes, energy comes! Wide awake till we come Matamoros." His laughter erupted. "You want? Come on. Good for you. Keep you high alert! Red alert! Ha, ha, like giving dog bone!"

I violently shook my head, and it felt like it was going to come right off.

"No? No? You no want? So be it! More for me." His laughter became a sheet of nauseating white noise. Then he began singing a hideous hymn to his pagan gods.

I must have passed out, because when I opened my eyes the blinding sun was high in the colorless sky. I immediately checked my lap. The leather bag was still there, my arms protectively draped over it. I was startled when I turned to look at Wendel, because there was a third person who'd shown up in the truck cab. She sat between us, and she looked like she was clad in sackcloth and ashes. Except her dress really wasn't that – it was an old, paisley hippie dress, and it looked like ashes because it was so dirty. Her hair was long, matted down in some spots, curly and a shiny black, peppered with grey patches. She smelled like she hadn't bathed in weeks. Her piercing green eyes bored into me, and I wondered if I was still hallucinating. Slowly her mouth contorted into a snaggle-toothed, gaping wide rictus. There was a necklace of dirty, yellow human teeth strung around her neck, peeking out from under the twisted strands of her hair.

"Oh, he awake now." Wendel laughed as if the very idea I'd been passed out was hilarious. "Only couple hours to go, Mr. Ray. Then Matamoros."

He saw me staring at the woman.

"This my sister, Marianna. We pick her up, last stop we make for gas. You no remember? No? No matter. Her son – my nephew – Alfonso, own small ranch not far Matamoros."

I was angry. "What was in that whiskey?"

"No, no get mad. Is okay."

"What the fuck was in that bottle beside liquor?"

He laughed, then she laughed, too. They conspiratorially glanced at each other and then back at me. Wendell shrugged. ""Silly-sideman' powder. It good for you."

"Silly sideman?"

"Si, Mr. Ray. Very silly, silly sideman," he moronically giggled.

"Psilocybin? Magic mushrooms?"

"Yeah, groovy feelings, no? Silly-sideman. Good stuff, you no think?

"You dirty fucker. You dirty rotten fucker."

"Why you mad? I no fucker. You say you like party. We have party in truck. Good time. Is good for you. No get mad at me, I do favor. Give you ride, give you party." He laughed.

I buried my face in my hands.

He reached over, handing me a medium-sized plastic bottle of unopened water. "Is okay, here. Take. Look. No open yet. Just water. Good for you."

I took it from him, twisted off the cap and downed about half of it without stopping. I felt my gorge rise, but I kept it down, and the nauseated inspiration to puke left me. It was broiling hot in the truck cab, and the air that was blowing in from the open windows was like standing in front of the maw of a blast furnace.

Things were a blur of blistering golden images in the brutal summer weather. Time swooped and whooshed, the hours disappearing into a long twilight of approaching night as we came to the ranch his nephew owned. It was a godforsaken place, a vibe of abandonment and decay emanating from the rotting timbers of the ranch house. Twenty yards or so behind it was another building, a long, low-to-the-ground rambling structure created from corroded, corrugated tin, worm-eaten wood and dirty, dented aluminum.

"Here is ranch. End of journey!"

"Drive me to the border, Wendel."

"Not now. Long in the saddle. Ass ache. Ass cramp."

"I need to go now."

"Ass ache so bad, my friend. We rest. My ass rests. Tomorrow morning, we go. I take you special."

"Can't you give me a ride now?"

"Only ten mile, but I too tired. Pills gone, I fall asleep soon. You walk, if you don't like."

I shook my head in frustration. My leg was killing me, and I knew I'd never make it on foot.

Old man Simon's words rang louder in my ears with each passing minute. His warning. There was something about the place. It reeked of – I didn't even want to admit it to myself then, it was too frightening – but it reeked of death. There was a faint odor in the air that I knew was decaying flesh. But every time I tried to figure out the direction from which it was coming, I was baffled. It would disappear as soon as I focused on it.

Marianna helped Wendel unload the artifacts from under the tarp in the bed of the truck. That was when a tall, handsome Indian-looking man with jet black mullet-styled hair – good Christ, another mullet! – came out of the ranch house with two shorter men trailing behind him. He was immaculately dressed in a pressed black shirt, black jeans and cowboy boots. The others were slobs, disheveled and stinking like Wendel and Marianna.

I scanned the yard, a weed-choked expanse of brown dirt and reddish sand. Several vehicles were parked between the house and the long, low-to-the-ground building – two late-model pickup trucks that looked virtually new and an orange 1980 Mustang.

Alfonso came right up to me, introducing himself. He spoke perfect English.

"You are a friend of old Simon, eh?"

I nodded.

"He is what many would call a good man. A good man, yes. He is always helping those less fortunate. Though it is hard for him to find too many less fortunate than him." He laughed, and the rest joined in with him.

Wendel sidled up to him. "Mr. Ray tired out. It such long drive." He laughed. "All our asses, they hurt!"

They all cackled again.

"I give him ride to the border morning time. After all have good sleep. Peaceful sleep, yes. Is good for you."

Alfonso and Marianna glanced at each other with what seemed, to me, secret knowledge, then both smiled. Alfonso put his hands on his hips in a haughty, authoritarian pose.

"Well, then, Mr. Ray must have a nice room in which to rest." He turned to Wendel. "Don't you agree?"

Wendel smiled strangely, his eyes sliding back and forth repeatedly, zeroing in on each of our faces. "Most certain, nephew. So courteous. Good for him. Good for all of us."

Alfonso made a theatrical sweep of his arm, ushering me towards the ranch house. I had no alternative. One thing I knew, before I fell asleep – something I was loathe to do – I needed to find a good hiding place for my small leather satchel.

Her name was Aurora. She was the closest thing that Alfonso had to a housekeeper. She clumsily introduced herself as she showed me down a long whitewashed hall. I couldn't understand her at first, and she had to spell her name out. She wasn't that old, maybe 25, only about 5'4", skinny, with a wavy black mane framing her high-cheekboned, Indian face. Once she opened the door to my room and ushered me in, I got a better look at her and realized she was attractive in an odd, unassuming way. I hadn't noticed at first because I was preoccupied, supremely weary of Wendel and his pals, and partly, I think, because there was a mask of fear that had frozen Aurora's features. She was frightened to death but, when I asked her what was wrong, she refused to say.

Before she left, she made some hand gestures, mimicking a creepy crawly thing with her fingers, pointing to my boots and saying, "Look out. Dangerous." She could only speak broken English.

"Scorpions?"

She vigorously jerked her head, and I nodded in reply.

After she left the room, and the door was shut – unfortunately it had no lock – I withdrew my .45 and tucked it under the mattress of the narrow bed. I wasn't sure what to do with the leather bag full of money. In the end, I decided to tuck it under the mattress as well.

The room had no windows, which made me nervous. A chamber pot and a pitcher of water sat on a battered chest of drawers.

Finally, exhausted and against my better judgment, I lay down. Lowering my head to the pillow, I decided it might be wise to check under it. Sure enough, I found a small scorpion, and I knocked it off into the corner, immediately crushing it beneath my boots. I decided not to take them off. Despite the adrenaline from finding the poisonous thing, I fell asleep. Nodding off – I didn't want to. Nightmares were getting greedy, tugging at me for more show and tell.

I was back, all the way back just halfway through high school. I'd only known Connie for a short while. We were going steady, but not all out serious. Not really seeing anyone else; still, we weren't making it into a big deal.

There we all were again...

That hellish summer, a lot like this one. I was out with Joe, a high school friend, no girls along, and we were wrecked. We ran into Fitz, his frizzy hair newly straightened into a big, oiled conk pompadour, like he was a cross between a glam-rock twink and a doo wop rockabilly. Joe made fun of him. He didn't like Fitz, not just because he was colored, but because he was colored with a pa who had money. And Fitz was ahead of him for a football scholarship, so that was a double whammy – though in the end, neither one made the grade. Fitz's pa was still alive then and protected by Mama, so Joe couldn't wail on him.

We were at Sleepy Eyes, what the locals called a hot-pillow joint. It was before Mama took it over. We weren't supposed to be there because we were underage. But the manager was too drunk to care. We were going to ball a couple bosomy blondes in itty-bitty negligees, and then Joe had to start in on Fitz's green sharkskin jacket. Saying he needed to head up to Macon in that outfit and find himself a fag bar. Things were getting ugly when a dork of a traveling salesman stumbled in by himself. Everyone around those parts hated traveling salesmen. Too many gullible dumb asses had been burned by shoddy merchandise, with no recourse later.

Joe homed in, transferring his bad temper to a more acceptable target. Fitz watched from the sidelines, and I was so wasted I had to sit down at a booth to focus. At first, Joe came on real friendly. The salesman was nervous but cocky – we were only teenagers.

"You all's just kids! What the hell's goin' on in this burg they let clean-cut boys like you in here?"

Joe put his arm around him, handing him a beer and steering him towards the back door. Fitz and I looked at each other like we knew we were going to see a show, so we'd better tag along.

"We ain't kids, Mister."

"You could've fooled me."

"Say, Homer, what you sellin' door-to-door to all these poor, gullible ladies?"

"Who's Homer?"

Joe smiled his wicked set of teeth. He pointed at the salesman with his bottle of Dixie.

"Me? My name ain't Homer. Name's Elkin. Out of Charlotte."

"You mighty long way from home – Homer."

Fitz joined in, "Yeah, Elkin, what you doin' down around here?"

Elkin was too drunk to notice till then that Fitz was black.

"Christ! What kind of a joint is this? Lettin' niggers in, too?" Then the sharkskin and conk hair registered. "And damn nigger queers from Chicago, to boot!"

Fitz suddenly had a meat cleaver in his hand. Joe shoved Elkin out the rear door.

I could barely walk, but I followed. There was a row of trailers out back – still are for that matter – where the girls take their johns. Beyond that was woods and marsh.

Elkin was stupid when he was drunk. A guy like him out on the road should've known better.

"Where we goin'?"

"Hell, Elkin, what you come down here for anyway." Joe smirked at him. "Pussy, am I right?"

Elkin looked over his shoulder at Fitz with the cleaver, then back at Joe. He laughed. "You bet your sweet ass!"

Joe laughed, too.

"Elkin, you ever hear of someone gettin' a Percy Mayfield?"

"A what?"

"A Percy Mayfield. You know."

"He some sort a singer? Somethin' like that?"

Joe nodded his head, smiling an evil smile. "Four stars for Elkin."

"What's that mean?"

Joe gritted his teeth as his grin widened. "Shee-it."

Blues singer Percy Mayfield had a big, dented scar in the middle of his forehead, rumored to have been from one of his wives nearly splitting his head in two with a hatchet. Though others said it wasn't any such thing, just a bad car accident.

"Elkin, you a traveling salesman, an' you never heard that expression before?"

"Givin' somebody a Percy Mayfield?"

Joe nodded.

Right before it happened, I had an inkling. But I thought, "Shit, no way. Joe isn't that crazy."

Real calm, not even breaking a sweat, Joe gently pried the meat cleaver from Fitz's fingers and, in a blurry flash, buried it in Elkin's face.

I puked by reflex, falling to my knees, only to find myself mere inches from the fallen Elkin's split-open, bloody, brain-spewing skull.

I glanced up at Fitz who'd just turned a shade green lighter than his sharkskin jacket.

Joe was already dragging Elkin by the ankles into the trees beyond the trailers.

"You boys," he hissed, "You ain't seen a thing, lessin' you wanna end up like ole Elkin here."

I awoke with the taste of dirt in my mouth and the smell of death filling the air around me. I couldn't see anything at first.

Struggling to sit up, I realized my hands were tied behind my back. I was no longer in the whitewashed guest room.

Fear coursed through me, stiffening my limbs.

I was in a very long, narrow chamber with a dirt floor. I was not in the ranch house but in the other building. To my right, there was nothing except a dim vision of tilled earth, an occasional mushroom sprouting from the damp soil. Directly in front of me were stacked rows of small rectangular parcels – drugs. I guessed coke.

I tried not to gag when I saw what was on my left. A naked, hacked-up, headless corpse – a man, I think – hung upside-down from a hook in the low ceiling. His torn-open throat dripped blood into a gigantic black kettle that bubbled over a low fire. It was a huge pot, like a witch's cauldron, and I recalled Wendel's talk about Palo Mayombe. Just beyond it, near the far wall, the corpse's mutilated, rotting head was stuck on a stake protruding from the ground. Its half-closed eyes blankly stared at its suspended body.

I'd never been scared enough to piss my pants before, but right then I came close. My stomach burned with adrenalinized anxiety. I tried to flex my fingers to tug loose the knots wrapping my wrists, but they were incredibly tight. My hands were numb from the cut-off circulation.

The double doors in the left corner nearest me were ajar, and there was the screech of a vehicle grinding and hurling gravel under its wheels. The motor switched off, and there was the creak and hiss of a cooling radiator. Immediately, there were the sounds of boots stumbling on the dry ground outside and the slamming of car doors.

Dusky orange twilight flooded in on me as Alfonso, Wendel

and their two nameless henchmen burst in. They were frog-marching a blonde, American teenage boy dressed in jeans, track shoes and a muddy letterman's jacket. His hands were tied behind his back, and he sobbed uncontrollably. He let out a startling shriek when he saw the horror show. Alfonso moved in front of him and slapped him hard across the face. The boy's face froze in a petrified mask of shock. Alfonso roughly took him, throwing him to the ground so he landed next to me. The boy tried to sit upright. I edged closer to him so he could use my body as leverage to get up off the ground.

"Oh, we are in luck. Mr. Ray is awake from his nap." He rubbed his hands together laughing, "Helping his countryman in a spirit of brotherly love. It warms the heart, does it not, my dear Wendel?"

Wendel's googly pop eyes wandered nervously around the room, and he shivered involuntarily as his eyes passed over the gory cadaver. Far from frightened, the presence of bloody death perversely displayed so openly gave him some kind of sick thrill. A leering smile grew on his face as he let his eyes roam over the boy and me.

"Nephew Alfonso, he has milk of human kindness in veins."

"Yes?"

"Yes, nourishing, dear nephew. We soon see, we soon taste. Good for you, good for all of us."

All four exited the building, with one of the nameless ones adding a couple pieces of wood to the fire under the cauldron before leaving.

The kid started bawling again. "Who are these fucking people? What the fuck do they want from us!"

"They're drug dealers, and they practice black magic."

The kid furtively glanced at the hanging corpse then quickly turned away.

"I don't want to die!"

"I don't want to, either." I turned my back to him. "Can you scoot along so your back is against mine? Maybe we can loosen the cords around our wrists."

We frantically tried, hoping our captors wouldn't pop in again at any second. But it was no use. The knots were too tight and our fingers too numb and restricted.

Then Alfonso and his posse returned, this time adding the witchy Marianna to the mix. She looked over at us with a wicked grin, sprinkled a handful of herblike ingredients into the bubbling pot, then took up a long wooden stake and stirred the viscous, foul-smelling brew. She barely turned her head to Alfonso and nodded. Alfonso, in turn, nodded at the two nameless henchmen who roughly took hold of the kid by both arms and dragged his struggling body towards the cauldron. He was screaming again.

Annoyed, Alfonso yelled, "Shut the fuck up, you gringo son-of-a-bitch!"

But the kid was beyond reaching, so Alfonso grabbed a long machete from Wendel. The two henchmen forcibly bent the kid over at the waist so his face was hovering only a foot above the noxious stew. Alfonso made a violent swipe with the blade, the kid's yells were cut short, and his head plopped into the cauldron. The nameless ones held his headless, twitching corpse like that, letting the heart pump out the rest of the blood so none of it went on the floor. I found myself hypnotized in shock, unable to turn away.

Suddenly there was a battle-cry scream, and the Indian housekeeper, Aurora, came in the half-open door, my .45 in her fist. Before anyone had time to react, she pumped a bullet into Alfonso's head with a deafening bang, and he slumped across the boiling pot. Marianna whirled, screaming, too, bloodlust in her animal eyes, brandishing her stirring stake, and Aurora fired again, hitting Marianna in the mouth so the back of her neck exploded, puffing up her scraggly, thick mane of hair. Aurora was trembling with energy and aimed at the remaining three men, who seemed to be in a state of shock. She yelled something at them in Spanish, and they all quickly sank to their knees with their hands up behind their heads.

She moved sideways to me and knelt, covering Wendel and the henchmen. All three were sweating buckets. Aurora struggled with the knots with her one free hand, and she miraculously got me untied. I stood with difficulty. I flexed my fingers to get the feeling back.

She gave me the gun, then picked up the machete that had fallen on the damp, moldy soil. Wendel went for the revolver in his waistband, but as soon as he tried to aim, Aurora swung the blade, cleaving Wendel's gun hand from his body. He yelled in agony and fell prone, the stump gushing crimson.

I stood over him. "Is good for you, no?" I looked up at the two grim-faced thugs that were left, stepping on Wendel's dismembered fist so I could pry loose the revolver. Then I had a gun in both hands.

Without any warning, Aurora plunged the tip of the machete into Wendel's chest. He let out a strangely surprised "Oomph!" from his sobbing, pale white mouth as it pierced his heart.

One of the henchmen dashed for the door, but Aurora was too fast for him, hacking into his spine with the blade, and he collapsed in a heap. The other one went ballistic, leaping on her back. I calmly walked over and shot him in his left ear.

All of them were dead. Aurora gestured with her dripping blade.

"They kill…*mi familia.*"

It was hard for me to believe that such a demonic crew existed in real life; it was like a horror movie.

I thought about stealing some of the coke for about two seconds before immediately realizing what a stupid idea it was. One, it'd be a huge risk taking it across the border; two, I could never live with profiting from it after seeing what had gone down in that tin-roofed slaughterhouse.

By then there were thick rivers of blood crisscrossing the moist, hardpacked soil of the earthen floor. Aurora and I couldn't help getting it on our feet, and as we walked out into the golden twilight, the red tracks of her shoes and my boots stood out on the dry dirt yard.

Once we were standing in the open, Aurora saw me eyeing the vehicles.

"Federales know them."

Then she had a good idea, showing me a closet where there were several dozen spray cans of grey primer, and we proceeded to quickly repaint the gaudy Mustang the color of dull ash. A terrible paint job, but fast-drying and good enough to get us over the border.

I retrieved my leather bag – still full of cash.

Things went by in a fast blur.

Once we got into Matamoros, it was almost dark. I found a side street that was comparatively quiet. I took a screwdriver from the glove compartment, and Aurora walked with me as a lookout. After ten or twelve cars, I found what I wanted – one with a Texas license plate. Before long, I had it off, then we were back with the American tags screwed on the Mustang.

Aurora huddled close to me like she was my woman, and we had no trouble getting over the border. The wait wasn't long, they passed us through without much of a second thought, and soon we were in Brownsville. But we didn't stop for another few hours until we got into New Orleans.

I gave Aurora five hundred dollars from the tiny satchel, and we parted ways.

I swerved back onto the interstate going east, headed in the general direction of home.

The car conked out on me in Mobile, where I got sick again. I ended up camped in a cheap motel a block from the bay for at least three weeks with a high fever. The clean warm air coming off the Gulf gradually helped rejuvenate me, though there was some kind of virus that lingered inside my gut, no matter how much time passed. I looked like death warmed over, but my appetite came back the last couple of days I was there, and I gorged myself on Creole seafood.

　　　　Finally, I picked up the Mustang from the garage where I'd left it – it only set me back another hundred – and got back on the road.

Then everything fell in on me again when I rolled into Mystic.

　　　　Mama filled me in about Red, Eli and Ennis "Mr. Raindrop" Lacey and the rest of the southwestern mob. It was a litany of woe that I couldn't believe I was solely responsible for generating. Fuck 'em. Mama didn't think that was a good attitude. She couldn't afford to feel, let alone act that way. She had to toe the line. After a good hour of arguing, she convinced me to hand over the satchel of what was left of the money. She left me a thousand as an afterthought, a pittance, and I resentfully took it. My feelings were that those pricks were not going to call off the contract on me no matter what they told her, so we might as well hold onto the dough and take our chances. But she didn't see it that way. Mama was one person I owed too much to and, in the end, I didn't feel I could go against her.

　　　　And then there was the bullshit with Connie.

　　　　One thing I did do was figure out a way of getting those Polaroids from Eli. Mama obviously hadn't known about them before and was not happy to hear of their existence or the part that corrupt DEA man, Harry, played in the whole scheme.

　　　　I couldn't believe it, but because of Eli's tie-in with Lacey and the mob, she was putting up the gnome-headed little psychopath right there in our own house. It made me want to retch. Every time I thought of him, I saw the bodies of Elise and the others he'd killed in Juarez, the Polaroid of his own bloody-faced father, Red, who he'd blown away without a second thought.

　　　　I asked Mama about the night pictures in the side yard by the cypress, the one with the gravediggers – her and Lucky and some other unidentified person. She became extremely upset and refused to talk about them.

　　　　Although Eli didn't sleep much, apparently when he did, he

had to be full of enormous amounts of liquor and drugs. Mama arranged it with Dolores, one of her girls, to service him in his room and slip him some chloral hydrate. Once we were sure he was out, we picked through everything he had. It took a while, but at last we found the pictures, tucked snug in the top pocket of a sport shirt. I plucked out the repulsive one of Connie sucking cock, and Mama kept the rest.

Before I left his room, I looked down on Eli – passed out on a single bed I'd slept on as a kid – and thought again how nice it would be to crush his head like a melon. He was even uglier than the last time I'd seen him, now somehow missing his eyebrows. Probably burned off from free-basing.

I sighed. Mama looked at me and grimaced, tugging me by my shirtsleeves out into the hall, then gently closing the door.

I refused to stay in the same house as Eli, so bunked with Jake in his big, rambling apartment above the garage, and I laid low.

What happened next was one of the most fucked-up things I'd been through. A few hours after I ran into Connie in the Milk Train parking lot, I found out Mama had sent her to New Orleans to deliver Lacey's share of my money. Supposedly, she'd be back in a week. Although I was filled with loathing for what Connie had become – and loathed myself for not mustering the guts to talk it out with her, I didn't wish her ill. And ill was all that I could see coming to her with Lacey and his crowd, despite her well-proven abilities to take care of herself.

Before I could get in touch with Janine, she showed up on her own at Jake's one night while Connie was gone. At first, I wasn't sure if it was Janine or her fucked-up twin, Jeannie, but then spotting her birthmark beauty spot, I was certain. Plus the sisters dressed different, with Jeannie not going in for the crushed velvet hiphuggers and hot pants that Janine favored.

I was drunk, lamenting my lost swag that I'd gone through so much to keep and lamenting my lost, betrayed love for Connie. Then Janine walked in, looking like a voluptuous banquet of sex, spilling out of her sheer, too-tiny tied-at-the-midriff blouse and impossibly skintight, blue velvet hot pants that left nothing to the imagination. Her long straight black hair was puffed up in front and cascaded halfway down her back. I should have known something was wrong. Connie and Janine were best friends, more like sisters to each other than Janine was to her own twin, Jeannie. But when she dropped by to see me, she began to trash Connie right off the bat. She knew I was drunk and that my resistance was low. I forgot about my heartache for Connie. Very soon she unbuckled my jeans and pulled them off. I was already shirtless because of the oppressive, wet heat of the night, and I tugged her blouse off, setting her breasts free. She crushed them against my chest as she pressed her mouth to mine and stuck her tongue down my throat. I had literally not been to bed with anyone since Connie, since we had had our farewell fuck the night before I was inducted. So I was primed.

Jake was passed out from bourbon and painkillers in the back bedroom. Janine and I went to town and around the world on that flimsy sofa bed out front. Once we'd finally had enough a couple of hours later, Janine dropped a bombshell as she dressed.

"Ray, you are one dumb, redneck motherfucker. You known the two of us all these godforsaken, motherfuckin' years, and your sorry ass still can't tell which of us is which. Just like a white dude. Poor pathetic peckerwood."

She took a washrag we'd just used to wipe off the sweat and cum and dabbed it on her high-boned cheek, rubbing vigorously till her "beauty spot" disappeared.

"Jeannie."

She gave me a cruel smile. "Got it right on the first try."

"Why?"

"Why? Because I hate you, I hate your lame girlfriend Connie and your queen bitch mother. Speaking of which, did Lorna tell you about me?"

"Tell me about you?"

Her resentful laughter echoed with depravity. "Yeah. You know? That I have the HIV. The fucked-up virus that brings on AIDS."

Chills ran through me, and I immediately sobered.

"Thought that would get your attention."

I sat up and pulled on my jeans.

"Of course, there's no guarantee you got infected. Though you really should've thought twice before fucking me in the ass without a rubber."

I couldn't talk. I just gave her a cold stare.

"And oh, yeah. Eli says hi. He's got the HIV, too. Probably picked it up in Juarez at some point." She laughed. "We been fuckin' since he got into town. Kind of dig him in a weird way, he is so damn ugly. Actually makes me wet." Her vindictive smile dissolved. "Be sure to 'member me to Lorna. Tell her what a good fuck I was."

She picked up her purse and sashayed out of the apartment. The screen door banged shut, and I listened to the clip-clop of her heels on the wooden stairs, then the asphalt yard. Soon her footsteps faded, and I was left staring at a shaft of moonlight spilling into the room.

PART FOUR
Lorna Diamond
August 1987

Chapter 21

Oh, my son, what have you brought down on me?

Ray is here, at last.

I'd already heard from Ennis and his people in Texas back in June about what my darling boy had pulled in El Paso. And I been working with my ass in a sling ever since to make his goddamn fuck-up right again.

I believe Ray when he says he didn't kill Red. It's not in his nature. I believe it was that little, sorry-ass prick, Eli. But that doesn't matter to Ennis and Broadstreet and Lucas and the rest. They don't give a damn about who really killed Red. All they care about is the money.

Eli – I never liked that boy from the first time I met him – what? – seven years ago? Right before he went into the Marines. How that sick kid ever made it in that outfit, I dunno. Probably because Red pulled strings. The USMC must've fallen on dark times.

Ray wasn't happy I sent Connie to deliver the payback money

to Ennis. And he doesn't know she's going to be gone for quite a while.

Christ, was I sick of her smart mouth and her getting into trouble. I have to admit, she is one of the few people I can trust. But her seeing that trigger-happy fool, Brody Van Heusen, blow away Fitzroy was the straw that broke the camel's back. Brody would've arranged for a little accident to happen, if I hadn't got her out of town for a while. Too bad she'll have to put out, apprenticing to Ennis for a year or so. Well, ole Ennis, Connie is the icing on the cake of our agreement. You owe me one, you slick, sorry-ass pimp bastard!

I'll get her back eventually, or maybe I'll let Ray do it, if he still wants her. He may not. He's all upset about her dancing for me at the Milk Train. I can't imagine what he's going to think once she's got a pedigree from Ennis. Of course, her coming back at all depends if she minds her P's and Q's, the sassy bitch.

Making matters worse, Ray threw me a real curve, filling me in on this connection between Eli and that fag DEA agent, Harry. Thank God we got back those Polaroids. What worries me is that there are surely more where they came from. The one of me and Lucky and Maggie Pyecroft burying her husband under the cypress out there in the side yard after she axed him in the head – that really took the fucking-A cake! Goddamn Maggie, dragging Lucky and me into that whole godawful thing. And now that ding-a-ling, Lucky, going and getting religion, following crazy Lester around like he's found a guru. Jesus H. Christ! When it rains, it pours.

What I'm worried about most is the money payback thing, if it's really going to be enough. I can just see Ennis keeping the contract out on Ray, out of pure spite. The only ones who're really standing in his way are Jim Broadstreet in Dallas and Del Lucas in Macon. If those two ever go, there's no telling what'll happen. Ennis and the rest have no loyalty to me.

Christ Almighty! I just got off the phone with Ennis, who was hot as a branding iron. Connie broke out, killing Billy 'Bilbo' Bannon in the process. Game over. She fucked me as well as Ennis.

I have to say, in some ways, I admire the girl. I really didn't think she had it in her.

But the whole house of cards is tumbling down.

Ennis never trusted me, and now it's worse. He didn't say it but, reading between the lines, Ray's back on the hit list. And I'm sure that now I am, too.

Just to play it safe, he let me know he'd called both Brody and

Eli about Connie. The girl'd be crazy to come back here to Mystic. But she very well might because of Ray.

Fuck, fuck FUCK! As if I needed more bad news. Now the writing's really on the wall. I just got a call from Brody. Steve Masterson, a state's attorney from Atlanta, is in the neighborhood, trying to be low-key, walking around in jeans and t-shirt like a good ole boy. Brody recognized him from a convention he was at last year. Brody says word around town is he's asking about Connie and Ray. Goddamn it. What the hell?

And more – Sonny Jessup came by to tell me that Lucky was seen in Moe's Diner having coffee with Masterson.

Soon as Sonny left my office, Eli materialized in front of me out of thin air. He heard everything Sonny said, but it wasn't news to him.

He goes, "Lorna, I don't think I need to tell you, we really got a house cleaning in order. I dearly hope you'll be enthusiastic about helping with the chores."

The nerve of the little prick.

Two hours later, Sonny checks in again, on the phone this time.

Lucky was strolling along with Lester on Overholt Road. Both were just killed, squashed flatter than raspberry pancakes by a fast-moving, late model car. Hit-and-run. No one saw the driver, but Sonny is positive it was Eli.

PART FIVE
Connie Eustace McQueen
August 1987

Chapter 22

I rolled into Mystic in the late afternoon. My arm was killing me, and my cast was falling apart. It was hard as hell to drive that way. No way I could've done it if the transmission hadn't been automatic. I was just going with the pain because it kept me awake, and it kept me white hot with the anger I needed to do what I had to do. Little did I know how much more that anger was to be stoked.

I drove sunk down low in the seat, my hair up and a pair of dark sunglasses shielding me from the prying eyes of provincial Mystic gossips.

When I rolled into my block, I thought at first I was in the wrong neighborhood. Then I realized what was off-kilter – our house was gone, totally destroyed, obliterated, razed to the ground. A barely standing, rickety skeleton of charred, blackened wood, melted glass, enamel and porcelain littered an ash-covered lot. I couldn't get out of the car for a good five minutes. I wasn't sure if I even *should* get out.

There was a statement there, shouting quietly in my face: "You are dead, your life is done here and you are history – ashes, like your house, the memory of your existence erased."

Fear was breathing down my neck, hot and sweaty.

Fuck them.

I slipped my feet into the sandals I'd bought at a convenience store, got out and gently shut the door behind me.

I stepped onto the rough carpet of damp ash and took a slow stroll through the ruins. My tread stirred tiny clouds of cinders that coated my ankles and legs. There were four gasoline cans, blackened and already starting to rust, plainly visible.

I wondered if Janine had survived.

I spotted the movement of something small and furtive in the backyard close to where my bedroom window had been.

I suddenly recognized Mur. I approached her carefully because she was understandably spooked. I crouched down when I got about three feet from her, and she took a running jump, leaping into my arms with a plaintive mew. I stroked her and held her close to my breast. Her fur was filthy, matted down with grease and ash. She cried softly, licking my face. She raised my spirits and strengthened my resolve in an unexplainable way. I carried her to the Malibu, gently set her down in the passenger seat, and then I fired up the ignition and, with a flash of inspiration, headed up the road into the woods.

I didn't stop till I got to the old Pyecroft place which, as I'd guessed, was still uninhabited, left exactly as it had been that night, except for the bodies being gone. I pulled the car out of sight into the open barn. It was a perfect refuge for the few hours I needed till I could put my plan into action.

Seeing the ruins of my house, on top of Ray's treatment of me, Lorna's betrayal and my killing Bilbo What's'is'name in New Orleans, had crystallized all the confusion inside of me and thrown up a mirror for me to look into, to see the reflection of my payback to them.

I found what I needed in the cellar of the Pyecroft house. It was hard searching at first because the electricity had been shut off, and I had to go on the hunt with a kerosene lamp. Something I had to be careful with, considering what I needed. But I found them down there – five full three-gallon cans of heating oil beside a cold furnace. Five of them, hoisted one by one, doing the best I could with one arm, dragging and carrying them up and loading them into the back seat of the Malibu.

Then I settled in to wait. I didn't have a watch, so I would have to turn on the engine occasionally to check the radio for the time.

Hopefully, if I dozed off, I'd wake well before dawn. I needed to wait until at least 4:00 AM before I could do what I needed to do.

I lay down on the front seat, curled up with Mur in my arms. Periodic swarms of mosquitoes zeroed in on me, but it was too fucking hot to shut the windows, so I thought I'd just have to live with them. After a few minutes, I couldn't take it anymore, so I went back into the house, found a bottle of vinegar and doused myself with it, knowing the tiny bastards hated the stuff. It worked, but Mur wouldn't sleep in my arms anymore because of the smell, preferring it outside on the hood of the car.

Sure enough, I soon drifted into a dreamless sleep. I woke with a start. There was someone or some thing rummaging around in the barn. Mur was standing, peering over the side, her tail erect. I poked my head out the passenger window in time to see the tail of a waddling skunk disappearing around the front end. I flipped on the ignition and tuned in the radio. I had to twirl the dial to find a station still on, then when I found one I had to listen to too many minutes of awful, new style country before the announcer condescended to tell me it was 3:28 AM.

Time to get ready. I went in the house and headed into the bathroom to piss. I was thinking of taking a shower to make myself more alert till I saw that no one had ever bothered to clean Ernie's blood out of the bathtub. It encrusted the enamel with a toxic film of reddish black poison, rich with a metallic smell that seemed to coat the inside of my lungs. I gagged as I flushed the toilet.

By the time I cruised into the Milk Train neighborhood, the roads were dead, the houses dark, and I saw nary a soul. The Milk Train lot was empty, and the building unlit. I pulled around to the far side, away from the road, trying to make sure the parked car would be as inconspicuous as possible.

It took me about ten minutes to pick the lock on the back kitchen door and another ten to carry in the heating oil. They always left a couple of beer lights on behind the bar. The names Dixie and Lowenbrau shone like beacons, giving me enough illumination to work. Heading around the counter, I had a notion to take a swig from the Jack Daniels on the shelf, but thought better of it. I hadn't had any booze or drugs in a couple of days. I was still kind of dope sick, and I craved drink, but I couldn't put it inside me. I was the most clear-headed I'd been in months and needed to stay that way.

I pried open the huge trapdoor at the far end of the counter, descended a few steps to turn on the bare bulb hanging over the stairs, then began hauling the cans down into the basement. I doused everything in that stock-filled cellar, then went over to the huge gas heater, kicking the metal accordion hose to the gas line until it finally sprung loose, spewing an invisible plume of rotting egg fumes all around me. I quickly bounded up the stairs, shut off the light and let the trapdoor fall shut with a bang. The way Mort and the other boys smoked like belching chimney stacks, I was certain things would start off with a bang when the place opened.

I made it out the rear exit and was just unlocking the car door when I heard a soft tread behind me, there was a sharp crack to the back of my skull, and I plunged into darkness.

I awoke on the lip of the Milk Train stage, sitting tied to a straightback wood chair, stripped of my clothes, a gag in my mouth. Blood was running into one eye and into my mouth. My bad arm throbbed with a pulse of hot pain that seemed to make my eyes bulge with each heartbeat.

Someone flipped on the house lights. Eli stood there nearest to me, with Jeannie, Mort and Sheriff Brody Van Heusen in a group a few paces behind him. Then this guy – I guess Harry, the DEA's bad penny – clad in a hideous maroon suit with a sky blue tie, waltzed over from the bar, a drink in each hand. It looked like straight sour mash, and he handed one to Eli.

"Our little Miss Muffett wasn't satisfied with her curds and whey. What you do that for, baby? Ennis was gonna take good care of you in the Big Easy. A direct pipeline of some of the best scag in the country right into your veins, and all you had to do was suck and fuck a cock now and then. You know, honey, my pal Brody here was for wasting you, but I got him to agree on a compromise. No need to kill somebody, right? Lorna and I worked out a little extra cream on top for Ennis when you brought him back the rest of that El Paso money, and he was only too happy to accept. Shame you had to go throw a monkeywrench into the whole shebang. Speaking of which, you use a wrench on ole Billy Bannon? I hear tell his head was all caved-in like an overripe cantaloupe."

He took a step closer and looked at my shredded cast.

"My mistake. There's old blood on that plaster, along with all the shiny, fresh stuff. Man, girl, that must've hurt walloping him in the head with that bad arm. But I have to hand it to you, it did the job. Better than I could've done, and that's a compliment."

He blinked his browless eyes a few times like he was

pitching a nervous fit, and his Adam's apple bobbed a couple of turkey-neck bobs as he turned to a nearby table. Jeannie picked up a handful of darts from the beer-stained top and plopped them into Eli's outstretched palm. He smiled his effortless death's head grin as he turned round to face me.

"Now we're gonna have a little fun with you, Connie. For all the extra trouble you caused us. And in memory of good ole boy, Billy 'Bilbo' Bannon."

He tossed a dart that pricked my left shoulder but bounced onto the stage.

"Damn, gonna have to throw harder if I wanna make 'em stick!"

He heaved another one, and it lodged like a nail in my stomach about an inch from my belly button. Brody chuckled and thoughtfully rubbed his five o'clock shadowed, liquor-flushed jaw with one calloused hand.

Eli handed a dart to Jeannie. She concentrated, hissed the word, "Cunt," at me, then let fly. The dart hit my cheek, puncturing flesh, drawing blood, sticking for a few seconds before gravity called and made it clatter to the floor.

The pain was surprisingly bearable, and I thought I must be numbing up. No tears flowed from my eyes, and I figured I must've cried myself out on my trip back and forth to New Orleans. Sons of bitches were not going to see me weep.

Eli handed a dart to Brody, but he waved it off, chortling, "No, you know what? I got a better idea. Something I been wanting to try out for a while. Be right back." He dodged excitedly out the front entrance, open now, and the twin screen doors slammed with a loud twang. Eli offered the dart to Mort, but he sheepishly shook his head.

"You squeamish? Goddamn pussy. Oh, well, don't make no difference," Eli commented, then whirled, hurling the dart so it stabbed into my right kneecap. That stung like fuck.

Excited Brody barged back in the doors with a longbow and a quiver of arrows.

Jeannie gasped in awe. "Sweet!"

Eli clapped Brody on the shoulder. "Gotta hand it to you, Mister. The law knows how to handle a two-timing bitch with style."

"This is it," I thought. Any second I was gonna meet my maker, if there was such a thing. I hiccoughed a sob, then got control of myself. No tears for these bastards.

Brody aimed, pulled the arrow back, then released.

There was an explosion of excruciating sharpness in my left thigh, as if I'd been bitten by a dog, and blood streamed out around the shaft that lodged there.

Jeannie and Mort had suddenly gotten a bit green, both retreating towards the doors. All at once, Sonny Jessup burst in. Strange, because no one heard his car. Then again, all of us were pretty distracted. Sonny had his gun drawn and slowly sidled up to Brody who was still turned towards me. Eli was oblivious, like he thought he was invulnerable. He smiled his death's head grin.

"What you think you doin', Van Heusen?"

Brody harrumphed indignantly, "That's not the way to speak to your betters, Sonny. Guess you're tired of your privileged position in our community."

"Shut up, you goddamn coward. A little graft among friends is one thing. All the killin' that's goin' on is another."

"I'll wager you probably talkin' to Masterson, that bureaucratic cocksucker, too."

Sonny smirked. "Maybe."

Then, through my blood-smeared sight and the shock that was starting to set in, I noticed Jeannie had snuck right up behind Sonny. She withdrew what looked like my .38 from the waistband of her bell bottoms and quickly hammered the butt into the back of Sonny's head. He crumpled. Brody turned and kicked him in the stomach. Then, at point blank range, he shot an arrow into Sonny's left temple. I screamed through my gag.

Eli whistled. "Phew! Good shootin,' Sheriff!"

Harry was not as up for all the blood and guts and queasily chimed in, "I'm going to go check around the lot."

"Yeah, you do that, Harry," Eli snorted with sarcasm as the Fed fumbled his way outside. "When you get back, come in through the kitchen door."

Eli then looked at Mort as Brody once again turned his attention to me. "Mort, ole buddy, ole pal, secure those front doors, will ya? Better to be safe than sorry. Next thing you know, this girl's beau, Ray, will be goin' all Sir Galahad on our asses and come gallopin' in."

Eli held out his hand to Brody, and Brody handed him the bow and an arrow.

"You ever done any archery, Eli? Ain't as easy as it looks."

Eli smirked a self-satisfied grin, then took his time aiming at me. He whispered, "Serves you right to suffer."

He let the bowstring go, and I heard the twang a split second after the arrow pierced my liver. A wave of unbearable nausea rose up through the sharp pain. I vomited blood on myself and felt as if I was going to pass out. No, I didn't want to go like that, fading into unconsciousness. I couldn't. I prayed some stray spark would happen to ignite the tinder box below us so I could witness all of them vanish with me.

Seconds seemed suddenly like hours. A haze of gauzy pink and red tapestries of ropy liquid snaked out of me. Paisley patterns of blood-drenched icons of dead, martyred saints from childhood prayer books materialized in a levitating tableau. I saw my parents disappear in an accordion of mangled automobile beneath a fierce locomotive; Ray lying on his deathbed, hideously burned and mortally wounded in the green votive light of his last refuge but managing to plug Jake and whisk his betrayer away with him; Billy "Bilbo" Bannon's head being crushed beneath my plaster-cast arm; and, last but not least, a giant mirror of my naked body, bound with rope and pierced with arrows, droplets of green fire licking at my toes.

Several giant, sparkly, star-spangled black camelias bloomed in the air around my head, then flashed white with a creamy iridescence I could taste – the sweet, salty consistency of cum.

As if in answer to my prayers, a chain reaction began.

Eli was frustrated, jaded from the dwindling catalogue of gory delights. "We gotta think of something else for our party girl here, don't you think? Don't want there to be a lull in the celebrations."

A light bulb went off over Jeannie's head. "Hey, Mort, there's a blowtorch down in the cellar, right?"

Eli laughed. "Now you're talkin', Jeannie! You're a girl after my own heart."

Mort was losing his nerve. The bloodshed was making the fat man grow pale under the fluorescent light.

"How about it, Mort? You know where it is?"

Mort looked at his feet and shuffled them, bashful all of a sudden. He shoved his hands in his pockets. "Ain't sure I know what she's talkin' about, Eli."

Eli exploded. "You goddamn tub o'lard, get on down there and look!" His anger suddenly turned to sadistic whimsy, and he laughed. "Shee–it, Connie! This is the kind of show you girls should be puttin' on here on a regular basis. We'd probably triple our business."

Eli glanced again at Mort, who was paralyzed with indecision.

"Hey, you damn walrus, didn't you hear what I said?"

Mort came out of his squeamish stupor and did as he was told.

He waddled behind the bar, then made a show of hefting up the trapdoor with difficulty.

"Goddamn, what's that smell?"

At that exact second, Brody took the opportunity to reward himself for torture well done with one of his Havana cigars. He snapped on his Zippo.

Someone started banging on the front doors. I heard Ray's shouting voice. "Open up! Open up, motherfuckers!"

"Phew!" Mort looked over the bar counter at Eli. "Stinks like rotten eggs."

Eli immediately guessed what was happening and whirled to look at me with furious shock.

I smiled through my bloody gag.

There was a heartwarming orange glow in the bloodcurdled room, then a long tongue of blue flame snaked out and away from Brody's lighter. It lashed out in a circular wall of fire that raced around the huge chamber, raging and white hot.

There was a blinding flash, then –

PART SIX
Janine Hickcock
August 1987

Chapter 23

Damn, I would have to get so drunk tonight.

Right when you need me most.

Am I always destined to fail the ones I love? Destined like all those around me.

Lorna calling Ray like some forlorn conscience from another lifetime had at last kicked-in, at long last dogged her, nagged her and chased her down...right as it was too goddamn, motherfucking late.

Connie...I knew something was wrong, honey. And here you are back after what I'm sure was Raindrop's hell.

I knew just from Ray's side of the phone conversation alone you're in trouble.

Now here I am beside him on this fucked-up steed of a Mustang as he races to save his lady love. Too late, always too late.

Is it?

I don't know, Connie, a bad, bad feeling is choking me up, baby, like a million metal stars are pricking my guts and boiling my blood. Like the honey river that runs between us has been polluted once too often by this poisonous place we call Home.

Connie, I asked Ray, not for the first time, "Why? How come you abandoned her when she needed you most?"

You know what? He gets all tongue-tied, like he can't speak. He tries to talk, but it won't come. There is some deep hurt in him, but it's a self-absorption that is hard for me to bear.

How *can* he? You and him, I was always so jealous what you two had...what you, I know, believe you two still have...

I think of Stevie, Danny, Hubie, Donna Marie and Massimo ... and you, Connie...you.

People I was in love with....or who were in love with me... but never at the same time. Someone always loving too much or not enough. Wrong time, wrong place...wrong life. One of us flying so high in the bluebird sky, the other crashing on the rocks below, wings melted from flying too close to the sun in this mad, bad, selfish, just plain unfriendly world...

We're coming, honey. We're nearly there...

PART SEVEN
Ray Diamond
August 1987

Chapter 24

Janine had been staying with me at Jake's after her and Connie's house burned down. I was out on the porch, the dawn not too far off, smoking a cigarette when she came out saying Mama was on the phone. I went in and reluctantly picked up the receiver. Mama immediately infected me with her anxiety, flooding me with panic. She'd debated whether or not to call, but her better nature had won out. Eli, Van Heusen and the rest had Connie prisoner out at the Milk Train, and she was sure things were going to go bad for her. I slammed down the phone, mad as hell. I grabbed my .45 and jumped down the steps three at a time. When I climbed into the Mustang, I found Janine inside.

"Don't even fuckin' say it, Ray. I'm goin' with you."

"So be it."

I popped in the key, the motor roared, and I rammed it into drive. I held my foot all the way down on the gas, and we shot out onto the highway towards the club.

There were several cars in the lot, including what looked like Van Heusen's and Jessup's black-and-whites. Agent Harry was leaning up against one, smoking, when we pulled in beside him. He backed away when he saw it was me getting out of the car. He reached inside his jacket, but I clipped him over the left ear with the .45 before he could draw his gun. He crumpled. I left him where he fell, and I raced to the front door, only to find it locked. It was a damn fool thing to do, but I started banging away at it, shouting for them to open up.

Then there was a deafening, thunderous bang and a white burst of instant incineration threw me into the air, away from the building and against one of the cars. I saw my clothes were on fire as Janine frantically dragged me into the middle of the lot. She yanked off her denim jacket and began whipping away at me, trying to smother the flames. Finally, in frustration, she fell on top of me and extinguished most of them.

She propped my head in her lap. Both of us were dumbstruck, unable to speak for many minutes, and we just watched, frozen, as the conflagration ate up The Milk Train, the center of it an alternately blue, white, then yellow sun.

Janine spotted something on the ground by my side, and she picked it up. It was the blowjob Polaroid of Connie.

"I'll be damned."

I was in shock from the explosion, and it suddenly dawned on me Connie was perishing inside there, right in the middle of that furnace, and there was nothing more I could do to save her. She was turning to ash as Janine studied the photo.

"I haven't seen this in I don't know how long."

My left side stung with the burns that were swelling up, but Janine's words jarred loose something inside of me. "You've seen that before?"

"It's my photo. Don't you remember?" She looked down at my question mark face. "I guess not. You were so drunk." Her eyes welled with tears as she gazed at the bonfire that was the club.

"What are you talking about?"

She wiped her eyes. "It's from at least three years ago. Not too long before you went in the Navy. We were all drinking and smoking and snorting, just the three of us, and she wanted me to take a picture, her going down on you..."

"That's me in the picture?"

She looked at me like I was nuts.

"Well, who did you think – ?"

Then she knew, and an expression of sadness and disgust came over her. "Oh, you goddamn *fool*. Where'd you get this? It disappeared about a year ago. After someone broke in."

"Eli and Harry had it."

"*This* is the big reason you were giving Connie the cold shoulder?"

I couldn't answer. My larynx and esophagus were tied in knots, and tears rolled down my cheeks.

"Oh, Ray, you fool. You poor damn fool."

She tore up the photo and let the pieces flutter to the ground along with the floating ashes and cinders. She squeezed my shoulder.

I glanced up at her, but she was staring at the blaze, her face wet from crying, and I lowered my head, filled with hot shame and regret.

Then I saw one of the cars was gone. Harry had come to and made good his escape.

The wail of Mystic's one, lone fire engine welled up out of the darkness.

Thank yous...

need to go out to Donna Lethal, Eve Golden, Byron Coley, Lili Dwight, Thurston Moore, Eddie Muller, Peter Maravelis, John Doe, Lydia Lunch, Grace Krilanovich, Mary Woronov, Jerry Stahl, Craig Clevenger, Alan K. Rode, Alex Maslansky, Liz Garo, Claudia Colodro, Billy Shire, Shepherd Stevenson, Benjamin Rew, Erika Wear, Dan Kusunoki, Mike Minky, Richard Modiano, Tosh Berman, Patrick Paepper at Alias Books East, Mark Rainey and Julia Smut

Chris D. is author of the novels *NO EVIL STAR, MOTHER'S WORRY, SHALLOW WATER, VOLCANO GIRLS, TIGHTROPE ON FIRE* and the collection *DRAGON WHEEL SPLENDOR AND OTHER LOVE STORIES OF VIOLENCE AND DREAD,*. His anthology *A MINUTE TO PRAY, A SECOND TO DIE*, a 500 page collection of selected short stories, excerpts from novels and scores of dream journal entries, as well as all of his poetry and song lyrics, was published in December 2009. His non-fiction *OUTLAW MASTERS OF JAPANESE FILM* was published by IB Tauris (distributed by Palgrave Macmillan in the USA) in 2005.

He saw release of his first feature film as director, *I PASS FOR HUMAN*, in 2004 (and its DVD release in 2006), and worked as a programmer at The American Cinematheque in Hollywood, California from 1999-2009.

Chris D. is also known as the singer/songwriter of the bands The Flesh Eaters, Divine Horsemen and Stone by Stone. He was an A&R rep and in-house producer at Slash Records/Ruby Records from 1980-1984.

His latest non-fiction work includes the mammoth 800 + pages *GUN AND SWORD: AN ENCYCLOPEDIA OF JAPANESE GANGSTER FILMS 1955-1980*

The year is 1987, and outlaw Ray Diamond's mother is the queenpin of crime in Mystic, GA. After his Navy discharge, Ray knocks over a mob-connected El Paso liquor store, not counting on Eli, the owner's psycho son, dogging his trail. Back home in Mystic, Ray's girl, Connie Eustace, resorts to stripping at Mama Lorna's club to make ends meet. Witness to a murder by the local sheriff, she goes on a drug-and-drink bender, jumping from the frying pain into the fire.

"...a crazy dive into a universe populated largely by monsters...a classic update of the Gold Medal/Lion Library loser noir tradition. Great work... "
– Byron Coley, writer for WIRE magazine, author of C'EST LA GUERRE: EARLY WRITINGS 1978-1983

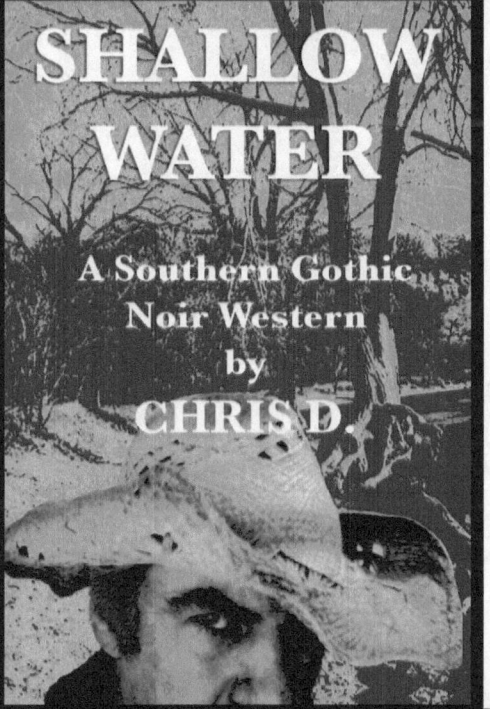

Post-Civil War, bitter rebel veteran and bounty hunter, Santo Brady, drifts through the Deep South. When he rescues halfbreed Indian prostitute, Lucy Damien, from one backwater town, he has the whole world fall in on his head. They embark on a freight-train-hopping odyssey to New Orleans, unaware that Lucy's rich white father and homicidal brother are tracking them. A tragic tall tale plunging head-first into a wild heart of darkness.

"One sinsister serpent of a story, an old Republic Pictures western serial scripted by James M. Cain and reimagined by Sam Peckinpah. I loved it."
– Eddie Muller, author of THE DISTANCE and SHADOW BOXER

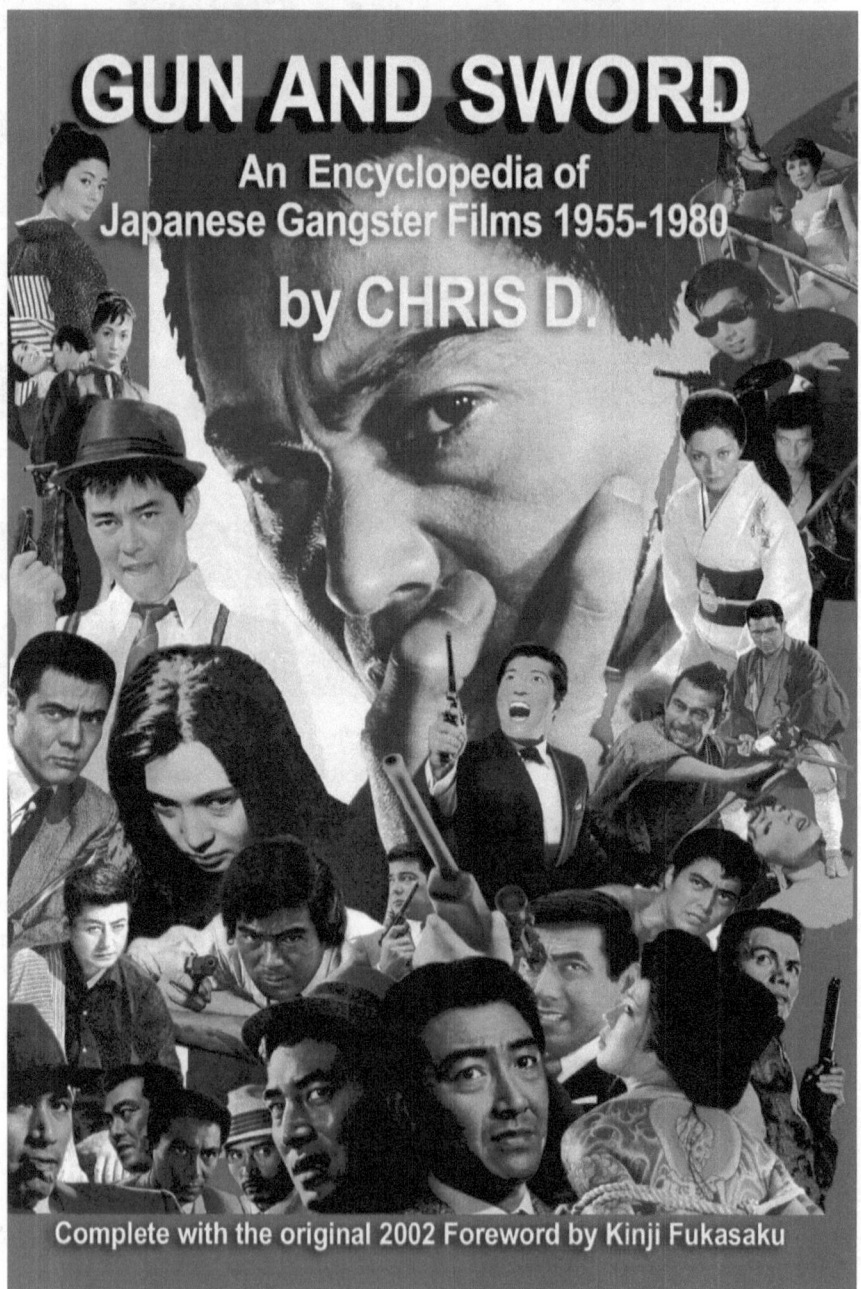

Two New Novels from Chris D.
Available October 2013

Half-sisters, schoolteacher Mona and junkie punk rocker Terri, are uneasy roommates while taking care of their sick mother. When their boyfriends, cop Johnny Cullen and killer Merle Chambers, clash due to labor struggles in their small town of Devil's River, the two women are pulled into the fray. To make matters worse, jealous female sheriff, Billie Travers, decides Mona is intruding on her faltering love affair, and quiet small town life amps up into an apocalyptic nightmare of uncontrollable violence and destruction.

Corrupt female police detective, Frankie Powers, is treading water in her small desert hometown of Sweet Home, California. Burned-out and emotionally numb after losing her husband and child in a mysterious fire ten years before, her conscience is reawakened when her affair with a Bakersfield narc brings new facts to light. Frankie's mob boss uncle, Jack Richman, has been kidnapping under-age girls for his Vegas prostitution syndicate; he's also been victimizing his own teen daughters, Frankie's twin bad girl cousins, Valerie and Vanessa. Soon Frankie finds herself singlehand-edly fighting tooth-and-nail against not only wicked uncle Jack but also his dominatrix wife, Marilyn and their degenerate hitman, Cal Nero. Can a lone shewolf survive against the bloodthirsty pack?

from **Poison Fang Books**